ON THE RUN

PUBLIC ENEMIES

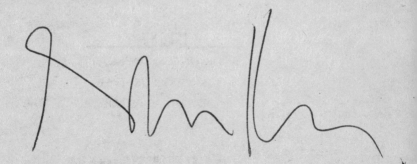

GORDON KORMAN TAKES YOU TO THE EDGE OF ADVENTURE

ON THE RUN

BOOK ONE: CHASING THE FALCONERS

BOOK TWO: THE FUGITIVE FACTOR

BOOK THREE: NOW YOU SEE THEM, NOW YOU DON'T

BOOK FOUR: THE STOWAWAY SOLUTION

BOOK FIVE: PUBLIC ENEMIES

DIVE

BOOK ONE: THE DISCOVERY

BOOK TWO: THE DEEP

BOOK THREE: THE DANGER

EVEREST

BOOK ONE: CONTEST

BOOK TWO: CLIMB

BOOK THREE: SNOWBLIND

ISLAND

BOOK ONE: SHIPWRECK

BOOK TWO: SURVIVAL

BOOK THREE: ESCAPE

www.SCHOLASTIC.com

www.GORDONKORMAN.com

GORDON KORMAN

ON THE RUN
CHASE #5

PUBLIC
ENEMIES

AN
APPLE
PAPERBACK

SCHOLASTIC INC.
New York   Toronto   London   Auckland   Sydney
Mexico City   New Delhi   Hong Kong   Buenos Aires

No part of this publication may be reproduced, stored in a retrieval system, or transmitted in any form or by any means, electronic, mechanical, photocopying, recording, or otherwise, without written permission of the publisher. For information regarding permission, write to Scholastic Inc., Attention: Permissions Department, 557 Broadway, New York, NY 10012.

ISBN 0-439-65140-9

Copyright © 2005 by Gordon Korman. All rights reserved. Published by Scholastic Inc. SCHOLASTIC and associated logos are trademarks and/or registered trademarks of Scholastic Inc.

12 11 10 9 8 7 6 5 4 3 2   5 6 7 8 9 10/0

Printed in the U.S.A.   40

First printing, December 2005

For Teri Lesesne,
college professor and motorcycle grandma

Thirty-one miles inland from the rugged Oregon coast, a deserted two-lane road was losing its battle to hold back the encroaching brush. The highway department had long since forgotten this lonely stretch, dozens of dreary miles from the nearest town.

It was the last place on earth anyone would expect to find an FBI agent at two o'clock in the morning.

Agent Emmanuel Harris squinted out the window of the police cruiser into the moonless gloom. "Why are we stopping?" he asked.

Sheriff Donnelly of Tillamook County, Oregon, was at the wheel. "According to the scanner, the cell-phone signal is coming from here."

Harris did a quick three-sixty. "I don't see the car."

"The technology doesn't lie," Donnelly insisted. "The car may not be here, but the phone is."

Wearily, Harris unfolded his towering six-foot-seven frame out of the car, taking care not to spill an enormous hot cup of coffee that had long since gone cold. He played his flashlight beam over the weeds and brambles. This was going to be like finding a needle in a haystack.

"Wait." The sheriff took out his own handset. "I've got a better idea. What's your number?"

When the ringer went off, it was so close that Harris jumped. He could even see the glow as the faceplate lit up. He reached down and retrieved his stolen phone from the tall grass.

He couldn't believe the image on the small screen.

It was the last picture taken by the camera function. It showed, in detailed close-up, a fifteen-year-old boy and his eleven-year-old sister: Aiden and Margaret Falconer, the fugitives who had been outrunning him, outsmarting him, and driving him insane for the past several weeks.

They were in a car — *his* rental car, stolen after they'd left him handcuffed and humiliated in a hospital room! This photo, taken by *his* phone, was their message to him, and not a very polite one at that.

Harris swallowed hard. He wasn't sure he deserved any better. After all, he had created these young outlaws by sending their parents to prison for life.

He snapped the flip phone shut. "Let's get back to the station. I want this picture on the front page of every newspaper tomorrow."

"What is it?" the sheriff asked.

Harris looked grim. "I think Aiden and Margaret Falconer have finally made their first mistake."

It was crossing the state line into Idaho that made Aiden decide he couldn't ignore the gas gauge any longer.

"Meg!" He nudged his sister, who was asleep in the passenger seat.

She was awake in an instant. "What?" No fugitive was a heavy sleeper. Life on the run had trained that out of her. "Where are we?"

"Idaho," Aiden replied. "I think it's time to ditch the car. Sun's up."

"But it's a million miles to Denver!" she protested. "How are we going to get there?"

"Not in this car," Aiden said firmly. "It's a rental stolen from an FBI agent. We're okay on back roads in the dead of night, but we won't last five minutes if the police give us a second look. Besides, we're running on fumes."

The reality of their predicament could not be denied. Buying gas was out of the question. Neither had any money — not one cent.

"We could always do the old fill-'n'-fly," Meg suggested hopefully. "We've already got every cop in the west after us. What's one more?"

"It won't be just one," Aiden argued. "Picture the report: two kids in a white Buick with Avis stickers and Oregon plates. How long would it take them to figure out that we're a lot more than just gas thieves? They'd surround us with roadblocks and come at us from all sides. The one thing we have going for us now is that nobody knows where we are."

The words were no sooner out of his mouth than a black-and-white police cruiser pulled off the shoulder behind them, lights flashing.

Terrified, Aiden checked the speedometer. Seventy-five.

Idiot! he cursed himself. They had escaped manhunts and had threaded their way through dragnets. How could he risk their freedom now by getting stopped for speeding?

He eased up on the accelerator and began to veer over onto the gravel.

Meg was horrified. "Are you nuts? What if he finds out who we are?"

"Shhh!" Aiden sat motionless, his eyes riveted to the side mirror. It was all he could do to keep from shaking as he watched the uniformed officer step out of the cruiser.

We're Mom and Dad's only hope to get out of prison, he thought desperately. *It can't end this way. . . .*

With measured steps, the man began to walk toward the Buick. Aiden monitored every millimeter of progress.

Closer . . . closer . . .

As the cop reached the back bumper of the rental, Aiden stomped on the pedal. The tires screamed against the dirt and stones, until the left front wheel grabbed pavement. The big car roared away, leaving the officer scrambling for his own vehicle.

Meg looked back. "He's coming after us, Aiden! Faster!"

Aiden whimpered with fear as the LOW FUEL light came on. But he knew he would run out of time before he ran out of gas.

No way I can win a race against a local cop on his own home turf!

Their only hope was to get lost — *now*! How could they manage that on a long, straight road with no turnoffs?

"He's gaining on us!" Meg cried frantically. "Do something!"

"It's a Buick, not a Lamborghini!" Aiden choked, keeping a death grip on the steering wheel as the speedometer needle vibrated past ninety. At fifteen years old, he had no license — not even a learner's permit. This was only his second attempt at driving. It was not the ideal time for a high-speed chase.

The tiny town was upon him so fast that he might have missed it. Slamming on the brakes, he wrenched the wheel in the direction of the intersection. But the forward momentum carried the car past the cross street. Suddenly, they were spinning around, out of control, pressed into their seats by centrifugal force. The Buick lurched to a halt in a cloud of dust, facing the highway.

Aiden opened his eyes just in time to see the cruiser flash by.

Now it was the policeman's turn to brake hard. As he tried to make a U-turn, a lumber truck, loaded with huge undressed logs, came by from the other direction, blocking his way and his view.

Aiden knew it was now or never. He drove straight across somebody's front yard and lurched onto the main street of the town.

Meg was chalk white. "He's coming any minute, Aiden! We've got to disappear!"

"I *know*!" But in this place? There was a lunch-eonette, a general store and post office, a bank, and a gas station with a car wash.

With his shoulders so tense they were up around his ears, Aiden pointed the Buick at the car wash and gunned the engine.

"What are you doing?" Meg was practically hysterical.

A front tire slipped into the slot on the conveyor chain.

"Put it in neutral!" shouted the attendant.

It was as if Aiden had spent every ounce of energy and will to get them this far. It was Meg who had to reach over and shift into neutral. The mechanism drew the vehicle into the washing tunnel. Water began to cascade down on the hood.

"You want hot wax?" the attendant yelled.

"Whatever takes the longest!" Meg called back.

Aiden looked out the rear window, dreading to see the police cruiser coming up behind them. The hanging rubber strips closed, blocking the daylight.

They were safe, but only for a couple of minutes.

"I hope you have a plan," Meg ventured nervously.

Amazingly, Aiden did.

Forty feet ahead, at the far end of the tunnel, was a dark panel truck, just about to enter the drying section.

It was their only chance. In a town this size, it wouldn't be long before the process of elimination led that cop to the one place he hadn't searched yet. There was no way they could leave this car wash in the Buick.

"Follow me." Aiden threw open the door and scrambled into a downpour of frigid soapy water. A giant rotating brush came out of nowhere and smacked him in the side of the head. He staggered against the car, reeling and spitting suds.

Meg grabbed his wrist, and the two ducked just in time to avoid an enormous spin-scrubber that swooped down on the Buick. They scampered forward through a drenching ice-cold rinse. They knew they had only a few seconds to traverse the tunnel before the car arrived to be doused with hot wax.

The panel truck's rear doors were only a few feet in front of them when a wind straight from a nightmare hurricane blasted into them, driving them back toward where the wax was now spraying. Shafts of light from the end of the tunnel indicated that the hood of the panel truck was already leaving the car wash.

With a superhuman effort, Aiden flung himself directly into the teeth of the dryer's gale and threw open one of the back doors of the truck. He and Meg clambered inside, the noise of their movements drowned out by the clatter of machinery. Aiden shut them inside, in total darkness.

"What if it had been locked?" Meg whispered, shivering.

"It wasn't." It was the most comfort he had to offer.

This was what their lives had become. Even when things went right, total disaster was never more than a hair away.

Tucked away in the windowless payload, they were unable to witness the dramatic ending to their narrow escape. When the panel truck drove away from the car wash, it passed the police officer, who stood waiting to arrest an empty Buick.

2

Meg hugged herself in the gloom of the payload. There was no torture quite like having no idea where they were headed. For all they knew, the driver could be taking them to the police this very minute.

Relax, she tried to calm herself. *If he knew someone was back here, he would have stopped by now to check it out.*

They were okay — for now.

"Hey, bro," she whispered to Aiden, "what are the odds that this guy's going to Denver?"

She felt rather than saw his grimace. "Slim to none," he answered. "But anything that takes us away from that town and that cop has got to be the right direction."

Meg nodded. "How far from Denver do you think we are?"

"Very," he replied glumly. "We'd just made it out of Oregon. I'm guessing close to a thousand miles."

It was a testament to how hard they'd fought that neither considered it impossible. A thousand miles with zero dollars for transportation or food? It was possible because it *had* to be. It was their only chance to prove their parents' innocence.

Doctors John and Louise Falconer were the husband and wife criminologists convicted of helping foreign terrorists. They had believed they were working for the CIA. In reality, they had been providing assistance to the Denver-based HORUS Global Group, a front for terrorists. That was why Denver was the next stop on this crazy marathon that had taken Aiden and Meg from Nebraska to Vermont to Los Angeles and up the Oregon coast. They had lost the trail of Frank Lindenauer, the CIA impostor who had framed their parents. Maybe they could find it again in the ashes of HORUS Global, Lindenauer's true employer.

"A thousand miles," Meg repeated, wringing some excess water from her T-shirt. "I wish we didn't have to do it soaking wet."

"Feels like we're slowing down," Aiden observed. "Be ready for anything. If he opens the back, we're going to have to make a run for it."

The truck came to a stop. The chassis rocked as

the driver climbed out, and they heard the slamming of the door.

Meg tensed. If they were going to be discovered, it would come in the next few seconds.

Nothing.

They waited — five minutes, then ten.

Meg strained to hear outside the metal walls.

No voices, no traffic noises. Not a sound.

The click of the latch seemed like a rifle shot as Aiden eased the door open. They peered out. They were parked on the dirt drive of a neat wood-frame farmhouse surrounded by rolling pastureland. The driver must have gone inside the house, because there was no one around.

Aiden and Meg climbed out of the truck and began to walk quickly down the drive toward the road. With each step, Meg expected cries of *Stop! Who are you? What are you doing here?* But it was as if they were two people alone in the world.

They reached the pavement and crossed to the opposite side, where some scrub brush would provide cover should they need it.

After all, Meg reminded herself, *we're only fifteen minutes from the car wash.*

She turned to her brother. "When our Buick

comes out all washed and empty, how long before they realize who we really are?"

Aiden was not optimistic. "How long does it take to type a license number into a police computer? This is bad news, Meg. They'll be watching all the roads. So unless we can walk to Denver one field at a time, we can't get out of here."

"We need to find some kind of ATV," Meg mused. "Like that quad we had in Vermont. We got halfway across the state without ever driving on a paved street."

Her brother nodded. "Too bad there aren't any ATVs around here."

A soft whinny reached their ears. Below them, in a gently sloping meadow, stood a big black plow horse with a white blaze on its forehead. It stopped grazing and examined them quizzically.

Meg's voice was full of wonder. "Look, bro — our ticket out!"

Aiden was wide-eyed. "You mean ride away from here? On *that*?"

"In the old days," Meg enthused, "that was an ATV. Look — it's even a quad. Count the legs."

"But we can't ride a horse!"

"*I* can," Meg shot back. "What did *you* do in camp all those summers?"

"It was science camp," Aiden said stiffly.

"Fine. I'll ride, and you design a particle accelerator." She grabbed his hand and dragged him down the slope.

He was still protesting. "But there's no saddle! No reins! We could fall off."

Meg was disgusted. "Are you serious? After all the stuff we've survived, your're telling me you're scared to get on a horse?"

He was tight-lipped. "Animals don't like me."

"I'll deal with the animal," she promised. "All you have to do is hang on. This is a gift, Aiden." She turned to the horse. "Aren't you, boy?"

In answer, the beast emitted a loud raspberry through flapping lips.

"See?" Meg announced triumphantly. "He looks friendly."

"He looks like a moose."

The horse allowed Meg to approach and stroke his flank. He regarded Aiden with suspicion but didn't seem to mind the young girl, even when she moved in front of him and began to pat his soft nose.

"Okay," she said to her brother. "Give me a boost."

"Are you sure about this, Meg? You're only a little kid. That animal could eat you. One buck and you're in orbit."

Classic Aiden, Meg thought. He knew this was totally necessary, but still he had to complain until the last second.

He took her small foot in cupped hands and heaved. She wrapped her arms around the powerful neck and pulled herself to a sitting position. Then she reached down and helped Aiden climb to the spot behind her.

She took a deep breath. Even she had to admit it was awfully high up.

"Here goes," she said.

She tried to jump-start the ride by squeezing with her knees. But this was an animal accustomed to pulling a plow. He didn't respond to riding commands. She tried slapping his flank with no result.

Aiden put his two cents in. "Don't you have to say *'giddyap'* or something?"

At the sound of the word, the big animal broke into a lumbering trot, heading for the pasture fence. There he stopped and waited patiently.

"Get down and open the gate!" Meg hissed.

Aiden was clamped on with a death grip. "What if he bolts?"

"This guy wouldn't bolt if you juiced him with rocket fuel! Look at his white whiskers. He's a grandfather!"

Gingerly, like he was descending an icy cliff, Aiden eased himself down to the ground and swung open the wire barrier. The horse moved through and patiently waited for Aiden to close the gate and climb back up.

Another "giddyap!" had them on their way, ambling over the scrubby high-desert terrain. They gave no thought to direction. So long as it was away from the town and out of sight of roads that might be patrolled by police, it was the right way.

They heard distant sirens a few times, chilling reminders that they were being hunted by trained and relentless professionals. Capture was never more than one mistake away. But as the hours went by, they never saw a single soul.

Meg clung to the horse's neck, "steering" by leaning to one side or the other. The endless rocking motion lulled her, causing her mind to wander. She and Aiden were already charged with arson, grand theft auto, breaking and entering, assaulting a police officer, and at least a dozen other crimes. Now they were horse thieves, too. What was next — cattle rustling? Wanted by the FBI, the juvenile authorities, and at least a dozen state and local police departments, should she now be looking over her shoulder for a good old-fashioned wild west posse?

They stopped only once, and it was not by design. They came upon a small pond, and the horse decided he was thirsty. Rather than be catapulted over his head into the water, they scrambled down, grateful for the chance to rest their weary bodies.

"How do the cowboys do it?" Aiden groaned. "I feel like I'll never sit again!"

But a few minutes later, they were back underway, rocking with the plodding motion of their mount.

They descended into shady valleys before the terrain rose again. Then it flattened into endless potato fields, still green with their fall crop.

"You know," said Meg, "I'm starting to have a lot of respect for this horse. He's not exactly a noble steed, but he's like the Energizer bunny — he keeps going and going." She grew serious. "I hope he can find his way home after this."

Aiden hastened to reassure her. "We'll never make hundreds of miles on this oat-burner. He'll still be close enough to his own farm that someone will recognize him eventually."

As they made their slow but steady progress, the sun grew heavy, sinking lower in the vast western sky.

"I think we might be coming to a town," Meg

observed. "Look." She squinted into the distance. "Four farmhouses. That's more than we've seen all day."

They trotted along, giving the homes a wide berth. Although they were many hours' travel from the town of their escape, the actual distance was probably no more than thirty miles. They could not rule out the possibility that people might be looking for them here, too.

A road appeared on the horizon. A couple of cars went by.

"Let's get away from here," Aiden advised.

"I'm trying," said his sister, leaning far to the right on the animal's neck. "He won't turn."

As the minutes went by, it became obvious that the horse had a destination in mind. No amount of pressure could redirect him, and nothing could stop him, not even a very loud "Whoa!"

They crossed two roads and then turned along a third, the horse accelerating to a full trot along the grassy shoulder.

Aiden was getting antsy. "We're going to have to jump, right? Is there some special way to do it?"

Meg's thoughts were elsewhere. "Do you hear music?" she asked. She snaked a hand into her pocket and pulled out a dainty pair of opera glasses that they'd been carrying around since LA. The left lens was now cracked, but the right could be used as a telescope. She held it up to her eye. "Uh-oh."

She was looking at a large cluster of tents, brightly colored fluttering flags, and milling crowds. The sun gleamed off rows of cars and pickup trucks parked in the adjacent field.

"What do you mean, 'uh-oh'?" Aiden asked warily.

"You know how we're supposed to keep away from people? I think we just found the county fair."

3

Meg handed the binoculars back to him, and he peered through the lens.

The horse broke into something approaching a canter.

"I don't see any cop cars," Aiden observed. "Maybe we could blend into the crowd. There's bound to be a lot of kids there."

"And do what?" Meg asked. "Ride the Tilt-a-Whirl?"

"We've got to hook up with some decent transportation. We can't take a horse all the way to Denver. There are whole mountain ranges between here and there. The Rockies, for one." He took a deep breath. "I think we have to go to this thing."

The horse thought so, too. For a while, Aiden was afraid he would gallop straight into the middle of the festivities, taking down tents and food stands in his enthusiasm. That would have called far too much attention to the young people who just happened to be riding him bareback. To their relief, though, their mount veered around the parking lot to a metropolis of livestock pens. He stopped before the horses' gate, waiting expectantly.

The Falconers dropped to the ground and let him inside.

Meg patted his flank as he moved past. "So long, old buddy. Thanks for the lift."

Aiden let out a sigh of relief. He was glad to see an end to the horseback phase of their journey. He grabbed his sister by the arm. "Let's disappear."

They rushed past the rows of paddocks and slipped into the crowded midway. The sudden switch from totally alone to completely surrounded was jarring and scary. Any one of these hundreds of faces might belong to the person who would end their freedom. All it would take would be a look of recognition and a cry of "Stop those kids!"

The tension threatened to overwhelm Aiden, and he struggled to keep his nerves under control. Falling to pieces would be more than embarrassing. It would be like wearing a neon sign that flashed CHECK OUT THIS TEENAGER.

Hiding in plain sight was a strategy, he reminded himself sternly. *If people don't expect to see you, they won't.* That line was straight out of *The Cyanide*

Capsule Defense. In addition to his job as a professor of criminology, Dr. John Falconer was the author of a series of detective novels. His hero, Mac Mulvey, was a master escape artist who believed that sometimes the best hiding place was right out in the open.

The food smells of the fair were enough to make any fugitive turn himself in. It had been almost twenty-four hours since either of them had eaten. True, food wasn't a priority when you were running for your life. But when the hunger hit — like now — it hit with a gnawing desperation that could not be denied.

Beside Aiden, Meg groaned, and he knew exactly why.

"Don't even think about it," he advised. "We're flat broke, remember?"

A second later she was grabbing his sleeve, pinching him through the fabric. "Yeah, but what about this?"

The sign read:

43RD ANNUAL OWYHEE COUNTY PIE-EATING CONTEST

ALL WELCOME

Aiden frowned, watching a procession of lumberjacks and Weight Watchers dropouts taking their places around the tables. "What are you talking about? We can't win a pie-eating contest."

"Probably not," she agreed, "but we can eat a heck of a lot of free pie."

He looked at his sister with respect. Meg could be illogical, impulsive, and sometimes downright crazy. But there were commonsense smarts to her thinking that geniuses couldn't match.

They slipped into the contestant line. "Don't make yourself sick," he advised in a whisper. "It's a long way to Denver."

They lost the contest, but the bloated comfort of a full stomach was so glorious that Aiden felt he now had the strength to move some of the mountains — both real and symbolic — that stood between them and the quest to help their parents.

Meg, too, was reenergized for action. "All right, bro. Now what?"

Aiden dropped his voice to a murmur. "There are a couple of buses in the parking lot. One of them said Boise."

"Boise? We're going to Denver."

"I know. But in a bigger town, there might be a chance to do a few odd jobs, make a few bucks.

Then we can buy Greyhound tickets and go to Denver without having to stow away."

They moved through the crowd, skirting the game booths, sand art, and temporary tattoos. They walked slowly because of the crush, but also to avoid attracting attention.

Just two kids enjoying the fair, Aiden thought. *That's us.*

Then the man in the shiny motorcycle helmet — the one who had been behind them since the pie-eating contest — turned left when they did.

Aiden felt his blood run cold. "Meg —"

"I see him," Meg confirmed. "Long blond hair sticking out of a black helmet. Think he's tailing us?"

Aiden steered them to the right around the cider stand. The black helmet followed.

"Could he be a cop?" Meg whispered.

Aiden shook his head. "Remember — the whole world's looking for us. There's a twenty-five-thousand-dollar reward for whoever brings us in."

"But how did he recognize us?" she wondered. "He wouldn't get much of a clean look in this mob, with our faces buried in pie."

The answer stared up at them from a garbage

can. It was a discarded copy of the *Boise Register*. Right smack in the middle of the tabloid's front page was a large color picture of Aiden at the wheel of the stolen Buick. Meg leaned into the frame, sticking her tongue out defiantly at the camera. It was the photograph Meg had taken last night with Emmanuel Harris's cell phone.

She froze, her face gray. "I've killed us!"

Aiden put an arm around her. "Keep walking. If we split up, we might be able to shake him."

She was shattered. "No!" The one thing his brave little sister feared was that the two of them might lose each other.

"It's just for a few minutes," he insisted. "We'll meet up in the parking lot. *Go!*"

She darted from his side and melted into the crowd. She was small enough to disappear immediately. Aiden had been counting on this. While Black Helmet's eyes were scanning for Meg, he dropped to a squat and tried to scamper off, hidden by the fair-goers around him. He was jostled and kicked as he doubled back against the flow of traffic. Weaving through the maze of bodies, he ducked into the exit door of the Haunted House.

It was a tame kiddie attraction, but Aiden was so anxious and keyed up that every cheesy ghost and vampire had his heart pummeling the underside of his rib cage. When he burst out the entrance on the opposite side, he had a clear path to the fair's front gate. He made for it, hardly daring to glance over his shoulder. Black Helmet was nowhere to be seen.

Safe — for now, anyway. But where was Meg?

"Aiden — over here." Meg appeared from behind a parked car.

He rushed over to join her. "There's the bus. If we climb into the luggage compartment —"

He was cut off by the roar of an unmuffled engine. A gleaming silver Harley-Davidson advanced slowly down the row of parked vehicles.

At the controls was Black Helmet.

4

These weeks on the run had put the Falconers' reflexes on a hair trigger. Their flight was instant. The motorcycle followed, closing the gap in a couple of seconds. Aiden could practically feel the heat of its engine.

"Jump!"

He and Meg dove between two cars, rolling on the brown grass.

The Harley executed a U-turn and lurched to a stop. "Give it up, you two," called a voice that was not entirely unfriendly. "I promise you won't get hurt."

"What do you want from us?" Aiden demanded, amazed to hear his own voice so steady.

"What do you think?" the cyclist shot back. "Twenty-five grand, that's what."

"Our parents are innocent!" blurted Meg.

"That's your problem," laughed Black Helmet. He gunned the engine.

With terrifying maneuverability, the machine wheeled on a dime, threading the needle between the two parked cars, barely an inch to spare on either side.

Frantically, Aiden and Meg threw themselves out of its path. They rolled over the hood of a big Ford and hit the turf on the other side. Stunned, Aiden looked up. The motorcycle charged again, its rider grinning with malice.

There was no time even for thought. In a split second, the hurtling machinery would be upon them. Aiden grabbed the chrome handle and pulled the Ford's heavy door open in front of them.

The crash was teeth-jarring. Black Helmet left his seat and smashed headfirst into the door, shattering the window with the force of his impact. The bike stopped, but the rider did not. He was thrown in an arcing somersault over the barrier, landing in a heap behind Aiden and Meg. The helmet rolled away.

Aiden steeled himself for hand-to-hand combat, but their attacker did not move.

Meg was frozen with shock. "Is he dead?"

Aiden knelt over the man and felt for a pulse. He found a strong, steady one. "He's in better shape than we would have been if he'd run us over. Come on, let's crack that luggage compartment. When he comes to, I want to be out of sight."

"Forget that!" Meg exclaimed. "We don't have to stow away on the bus. We've got wheels!"

"What — the motorcycle?" Aiden regarded the big Harley, leaning against the Ford. It seemed undamaged, but — "I can't drive that monster!"

She glared at him. "If there's one thing I've learned since we left Sunnydale Farm, it's that you can do anything."

Aiden gulped. Was his sister so naive that she actually believed that? Didn't she see that all his heroics of the past weeks had been a mixture of desperation and pure luck?

The Harley weighed a ton. He barely had the strength to wrestle it fully upright and swing his leg over the seat. It was still idling, which was a good sign. All his motorcycle knowledge came from TV. Wasn't the throttle on the handlebar? He gave the right one a slight twist and worked up enough forward momentum to move out from between the parked cars. Then he turned to the left and made an experimental run down the field. The acceleration of the bike was scary, like a force of nature was pushing from the rear.

Meg came running up behind him. "Hey — wait for me!"

Aiden squeezed the front brake, and the Harley stopped so suddenly that he almost went the way of the previous rider.

Meg picked up the shiny black helmet and handed it to her brother. There was a smaller one clipped on behind the seat. This she put on herself. "Practice on the road," she said, climbing on behind him. "When somebody finds that jerk, we want to be ancient history."

Driving the Harley was like straddling a rocket to the moon. The speed was dizzying. Even when the speedometer only showed fifty, the hurricane-force winds blasting by threatened to hurl driver and passenger off into space. The slightest pressure on the gas produced an instant spurt of acceleration that left their hearts and stomachs behind.

"This is awesome, bro!" Meg had to bellow directly into his helmet to be heard over the earsplitting roar of the motor. "It's the only way to travel!"

Leave it to Meg to be having a good time while he was barely managing to keep them upright and alive. She was hanging on with one arm while fumbling to unfold a road map from the seat-side pouch. It billowed like the mainsail of a schooner in a full gale.

They took local roads away from the fair, following signs for Boise. Just before the interstate, Aiden pulled over at a police phone box. "There's a man lying in the parking lot of the Owyhee County fair," Aiden told the operator in his deepest voice. "I think he's been hurt." He hung up before the woman could ask any questions.

On the highway, Aiden gradually developed some confidence on the Harley. But he never got used to the curves. The bike would tilt forty-five degrees on every bend in the pavement. It was a spine-chilling reminder — they were traveling at car velocity, minus the protection of tons of metal around them.

Wipe out on this thing and you're instant roadkill.

As they followed the Interstate toward Utah, Aiden's eyes drifted to the gas gauge. He managed to ignore it for a while. But when the needle was touching the red *E*, he pulled off at the next exit.

"What's the matter?" Meg called from behind.

"Gas."

Different vehicle, same dilemma. With no money, buying gas was not an option. They had to steal it. But to fill-'n'-fly at the station at the turnoff wasn't an option. There would be cameras at the pumps. That would be like handing the police a calling card, telling them where to look *and* what to look for.

Aiden drove down the road, racking his brain for some sort of plan. The digital clock on the minimart read 9:48 P.M. — not exactly the middle of the night. But in sleepy rural country, most people were probably inside for the evening.

When he spotted the farmhouse, he knew it was the right place. It had a separate garage out of sight of the residence.

"Why are we stopping way out here?" asked Meg.

"You think people won't notice a Harley-Davidson motorcycle revving on their lawn? We'll walk it the rest of the way."

Each took a handlebar and they rolled the bike along the dirt drive. With no forward momentum, the six-hundred-pound piece of machinery was heavy and awkward.

Under cover of a stand of desert pines, Aiden squinted in the moonlight. "Look," he said. A John Deere riding mower was parked outside the prefab aluminum barn. "That thing runs on gas. Which means there should be a fuel can around here somewhere."

As it turned out, the household had several gas vehicles, including a jet ski, a snowmobile, and a Honda motorcycle that was almost as big as the Harley. Two five-gallon cans sat side by side on a high shelf next to some roofing shingles.

Aiden was surprised how easy it was to fill the Harley's tank. It took less than a single canister. He replaced the cap and looked down to see Meg on her hands and knees with a screwdriver, removing the motorcycle's license plate.

"What are you doing?"

"Switching plates with the other bike," she explained. "That way, if a cop feeds our license number into his computer, it won't come up as stolen."

"Good idea," Aiden said, impessed. "Let's hit the road."

They were pushing a Harley back up the drive when they heard a rustling sound.

"What's that?" hissed Meg.

They froze, their ears filtering out the traffic noise from the freeway. There it was — a faint swishing, mixed with the crackling of twigs.

Someone — or something — was stalking them.

5

Meg looked around anxiously. "Police?" she whispered.

Aiden shook his head. "They don't hide; they just arrest you." He kept his real fear to himself — a guard dog. A Doberman, shepherd, or pit bull following them through the bushes, preparing to pounce —

Keep moving. You're almost at the road. . . .

"Now!" He jumped onto the Harley and helped the much shorter Meg swing her leg over the saddle.

There was an odd honk, accompanied by a wild flapping sound. Aiden felt a rush of air. A scream was torn from his sister's throat.

"Meg — " He wheeled to face their attacker.

An enormous white goose hung in the air over Meg, battering her head and shoulders with its three-foot wingspan. Aiden reached back to swat the big bird away. It clamped its powerful beak onto his middle finger.

"Ow!"

He shook his hand, but the ill-tempered fowl would not let go. Heavy wings slapped against his face. At close range, the honking was deafening. An upstairs light came on in the farmhouse.

He felt a stab of fear. *This bird might as well be a mountain lion if it gets us caught!*

Not knowing what else to do, he turned the key and brought his left foot down on the kick start. The Harley roared to life. He squeezed the clutch and nudged the gearshift into first with the toe of his sneaker. But when he twisted the throttle, the engine sputtered and died.

Enraged by the sudden burst of noise, the goose began pecking at his face.

Flustered, Aiden tried again. This time, the bike lurched forward a few feet before stalling out.

"What's the problem?" Meg hissed, swiping at the blizzard of white feathers.

"I can't start this thing!"

"What are you talking about?" she demanded. "We've been riding for hours!"

"Yeah, but it was already going then!" he explained desperately. "We never started it up before!"

Now the porch light was on, too. A figure peered

out the window in the door, straining to see what was going on.

Meg recoiled from a jab from the goose. "You'd better learn pronto, or we're going to have a lot more to worry about than a stupid bird!"

Fighting panic, Aiden released the clutch, gently rolling the accelerator. When the motor didn't stall, he wrenched the throttle. The Harley leaped away from the farmhouse in a dizzying burst of raw power. The goose hung on for a few seconds and then flew off the bike, disappearing into the night.

They were back on the expressway in less than a minute. A slipstream of feathers and down blew off them for the next mile and a half.

Meg laughed at the comet tail of fuzz, and even Aiden cracked a smile. But in a world where a barnyard fowl with a bad attitude could threaten their quest, nothing was very funny.

The drive to Denver took all night, with two more nerve-racking fuel heists — one in Utah and one in Wyoming. The air grew cooler, and the windchill on the speeding motorcycle felt like the North Pole. Actually, Aiden welcomed the steady blasting cold. He hadn't slept in close to two days, and fatigue threatened to overpower him. A few times, he felt his sister's arms relax around his midsection, and he had to pull over and wake her up. If she ever fell completely asleep, she'd be blown clear off the bike.

Dawn found them just over the Colorado State line, heading south on I-25 toward Denver. They pulled over at the entrance to a state recreation area, where a pipe bubbled with clear, frigid water straight from a mountain spring. The Falconers drank their fill and washed their faces. They were exhausted beyond imagination, and the gnawing hunger pangs had returned. But at least they felt alive again.

Up ahead, a sign declared DENVER 74.

Meg wore a big smile. "We made it, bro. HORUS Global, here we come."

Aiden marveled at her optimism. How different could a brother and sister be? His own thinking was exactly this: *If we can't pick up Frank Lindenauer's trail in what's left of HORUS, we've got no place else to go. We'll be dead in the water.*

It would be the end of the road for the Falconer family.

6

They hit the city at morning rush hour and crawled into town amid heavy traffic. There was no way to escape the hundreds of pairs of eyes taking in the sight of two kids on a Harley. Aiden was tall enough to pass for an adult, but not Meg, who was shorter, with a slight build. At least the helmets obscured their faces.

They turned off the highway and began to explore the neighborhoods north of downtown. They had decided to stop at the first library they found. True, any public place was risky for fugitives. But there were advantages, too. Strangers were welcomed at a library, not questioned. Study cubicles and other nooks and crannies made it easy to keep a low profile. And there were busy parking lots where a certain Harley-Davidson motorcycle might stand out a little less.

Most of all, libraries had *information*. The Falconers had never been to Denver in their lives. They knew next to nothing about HORUS Global Group. A library would have maps, atlases, Internet access. It was the ideal place to begin this next phase of their search.

The Hillsdale branch of the Denver Public Library was in an older section of the city, surrounded by small apartment buildings and modest homes. They tucked the bike into the shadows between two big SUVs and entered the building.

It could have been any library anywhere — endless metal shelving, institutional furniture, and the Dewey decimal system. To Meg, one feature stood out above all others.

"A *real* bathroom!" she whispered longingly. "Find a spot. I'll be right back." She hurried off down the hall.

Aiden selected an isolated cubicle hidden in the 700s and took his place in the stiff-backed chair. There he sat, yawning wide enough to drive a truck through. Funny — he'd been totally exhausted for most of the past two days. But now — in this momentary reprieve from the chase — the full weight of his fatigue landed right on top of him.

Cut it out, he ordered himself. *You're too busy to be tired.*

From his pockets he pulled a series of folded, dog-eared papers, faded and ruined, waterlogged and dried out several times over. It was all the information they had on Frank Lindenauer. Any chance of getting their parents out of prison depended on this collection of pulpy scraps.

There were a few faxes that had come from Mom and Dad's lawyers, a flyer from a charity run by HORUS, and an old vacation snapshot of the family friend Aiden had once called Uncle Frank.

He turned his attention to the faxes first. The ink was so smeared and washed out that the documents were barely readable. He searched for important names like HORUS or Lindenauer, but nothing jumped out at him.

The printing had held up a little better on the flyer, but so what? What did they need to know about a fake charity set up by HORUS to funnel money to terrorists? The East Asian Children's Charitable Fund wasn't even based in Denver. Their offices had been in California.

And then he saw it, in fine print on the back of the leaflet:

CHARITABLE STATUS CERTIFICATE AVAILABLE UPON WRITTEN REQUEST TO:
Donor Services

HORUS Global Group
Suite 1108 — Denver Executive Center North
2700 Federal Avenue
Denver, CO 80281

That was it — HORUS headquarters! True, the organization had been shut down for more than a year. But it was a place to start.

As long as there's a clue to follow, a stone left unturned, there's still hope for Mom and Dad.

One wall of the reference area was taken up with a huge Denver city map. It was a simple matter to plot a course from the Hillsdale Branch to Federal Avenue. They'd leave the minute Meg —

He frowned. Where *was* Meg? In all the excitement of his discovery, his sister had completely slipped his mind. According to the clock, she'd been gone for half an hour. How long did it take to go to the bathroom?

Could she be wandering through the library, looking for me?

He searched every inch of the Hillsdale branch.

Meg was nowhere to be found.

7

Worst-case scenarios spun out of control inside Aiden's head: Meg had been recognized and had climbed out the bathroom window to make a run for it. Or worse — she'd been captured and dragged in to the cops for the reward money. What if she was lying on the lavatory floor, in desperate need of medical attention? It took every ounce of willpower Aiden had to keep himself from charging in to help her.

That would be a great way to help Mom and Dad — by getting arrested for storming the ladies' room.

The first sight of her faded sneaker stepping through the door brought him such a measure of relief and rage it was all he could do from running over and shaking her. The words were already formed in his mouth: *Are you out of your mind? I tore this building apart looking for —*

Then she came into view, and the heart that had been about to jump through his rib cage melted into slush. Her face was flushed, her eyes squinty and blinking rapidly.

She had fallen asleep!

In his crushing exhaustion, it had never occurred to him that Meg must be every bit as tired as he was. Horrible as all this was for Aiden, at least he was fifteen, man-size and approaching adulthood. His sister was just a kid.

"I didn't do it on purpose," she pouted apologetically.

"It's okay," he soothed. "Listen — I found HORUS. I know where their offices used to be."

A bucket of ice water could not have brought her to such instant alertness. "What are we waiting for?"

"Well —" He looked sheepish. "I'm pretty much dead on my feet. And since you've already proved it's possible to sleep on a toilet seat —"

She favored him with a smile. "If you're not back in an hour, I'll pull the fire alarm."

Meg could feel the librarian's eyes upon her. She was sure of it — almost like the tingling of Spider-Man's spider sense.

Fugitives know when they're being watched.

Sure enough, the young woman was walking toward her.

Meg closed the newspaper and rushed to return it to the periodical shelves. That would be perfect — to be nabbed while reading an article about herself and Aiden headlined PUBLIC ENEMIES NUMBER ONE AND TWO?

She snuck a glance over her shoulder. The librarian was only a few feet away.

Should I run for it?

No — not with Aiden sacked out in the men's room. She had no choice but to bluff through it.

"Hi, there," the woman greeted. "Is there something I can help you with?"

"Oh, no, thanks," Meg replied casually. "I'm cool."

The librarian smiled awkwardly. "I suppose what I really mean is — well, shouldn't a girl your age be in school right now?"

The flood of relief nearly knocked Meg over. She was caught, all right — not for being a fugitive, but for ditching class!

"I'm homeschooled," she said smoothly. Meg was never at a loss for an excuse under pressure. "Mom sent me to work on my current events project. She's a stickler for the state curriculum."

That seemed to satisfy the librarian. Still, Meg decided to make herself scarce for a while. She followed a sign that read TEEN SCENE to Hillsdale's young adult section in the basement. It had a very different feel from the rest of the branch — not as stuffy and quiet. A radio was playing softly.

There were newspapers here, too, and Meg picked up a copy of the *Rocky Mountain News*. Luckily, their picture had disappeared off the front page. What an idiot she had been to take that photo on Agent Harris's cell phone! Before, the police had known them only through mug shots that were almost a year old. Now she'd given the whole world a clear view of exactly what they looked like today.

Stupid, stupid, stupid!

Aiden could be a wimp sometimes, but at least he thought before he acted. Her brother never would have made a crazy, impulsive blunder like that.

According to the *Rocky Mountain News*, nobody knew they were in Denver. Still, it was scary to see how quickly the cops could put two and two together. They had already connected the abandoned rental car in the car wash with the borrowed plow horse — which had turned up at the very same fall fair where a certain Harley-Davidson motorcycle had been stolen.

At least the horse made it home okay. And even Black Helmet got away with a concussion, the jerk.

So the authorities were searching for a Harley, but they had the wrong license number. As far as the police were concerned, Aiden and Meg could be anywhere within a thousand miles of the Owyhee County fair. The FBI was even considering the possibility that they had crossed the border into Canada. Now the Royal Canadian Mounted Police were looking for them, too.

They'd lost the cops. They had a fresh lead on HORUS. Could it be that things were finally starting to look up?

And then a voice announced, "I say they take those criminal *brats*, stick 'em in a cell with their terrorist parents, and throw away the key!"

8

Meg tensed. Was there an enemy close by?

Her eyes fell on the radio, and she realized why the voice was so familiar. Someone was listening to the Mouth of America, the notorious shock jock. No Falconer could ever forget his in-your-face New York accent. Back in the days of Mom and Dad's trial, the Mouth had been one of the loudest of the Falconer haters. He had even pushed for the husband and wife criminologists to be given the death penalty.

"And here's another thing that rots my socks!" Every word uttered by the Mouth was shouted, as if in the heat of argument. "The juvenile justice system. That's just another way of saying it's okay to let kids get away with murder while the rest of us fry. Scrap the whole thing. A crime is a crime is a crime. Ohio — you're on the air."

"Hi, Mouth," came a woman's voice. "Longtime listener, first-time caller."

The shock jock was obnoxious. "You got something to say, or should I grab a nap here?"

"Well, I'm the mother of a teenager, and I'm not sure fifteen — let alone eleven — is old enough to understand the consequences —"

"What planet do you live on, lady?" the Mouth interrupted belligerently. "They handcuffed a federal agent to a radiator! They stole a car! And a motorcycle! What difference does it make if they're fifteen or thirty-five or ninety-five? You break the law, you pay the price. These rotten kids should have to pay just the same as their parents. That's how I see it! You got a problem with that? Call me at 1-800-US-MOUTH. I'll set you straight."

Meg's jaw stiffened. What did that big windbag know about justice? As if being a desperate fugitive was a *choice*, like signing up for soccer or joining the Girl Scouts! Nobody ever took the Mouth's family and tore it to pieces!

All at once, she was marching back up the stairs to the bank of pay phones near the front entrance. She punched in the number with a finger like a jackhammer and was almost surprised when the keypad didn't shatter — 1-800-US-MOUTH.

She counted twenty-six rings but hung in there, burning to have her say.

"Mouth Line," an operator answered at last. "What's your beef?"

"Just put me on the radio," Meg said.

The man was dubious. "How old are you — ten?"

"Eleven," she corrected. "I'm Meg Falconer."

There was a pause. "And you can prove that?"

"Nobody else pretends to be me," Meg informed him icily. "It isn't that fun."

There was a flurry of activity on the other end of the connection, followed by a whispered argument. The next voice she heard belonged to the Mouth himself.

"Well, according to the control room, today's show has a special guest star. Margaret Falconer — can you hear me?"

On the air with the shock jock and his radio audience of millions, Meg felt her courage deserting her. In that instant, her elaborate plans to give this blowhard a piece of her mind evaporated, and she could barely manage a whispered, "That's Meg."

The Mouth didn't hear her. "Margaret, are you on the line?"

"Meg," she said, louder this time. "People call me Meg."

"All right, Meg — if that's who you really are. Now, exactly where are you and your brother right now?"

"Do you think I'm stupid?" snapped Meg. "The FBI could be listening."

"Right." The shock jock's voice dripped with sarcasm. "We can't have the big bad police scaring the poor innocent kiddies. Since when is it wrong for the cops to arrest criminals? Because that's what you are — criminals. That's how I see it. You got a problem with that?"

"Yeah, I've got a problem with that," Meg retorted. "We hadn't done a single thing wrong when they stuck us on a prison farm."

"Which your brother burned to the ground."

"That was an *accident*!"

The Mouth snorted. "Pretty convenient accident."

"That farm was run like the Stone Age. They send you out to a barn full of hay with a kerosene lamp. If they'd given us flashlights, the place would still be standing."

"That doesn't explain the cars you stole, the ATV, and the motorcycle," the shock jock persisted. "That doesn't explain breaking and entering, destruction of property, and stowing away. That doesn't explain assaulting a federal agent."

"Every time we broke the law, it was because we had no choice," Meg said righteously. "It was either that or get caught."

"That's no excuse!" the Mouth stormed. "That's like saying if you rob a bank, it's okay to shoot at the cops because they're chasing you! It's time for you and your brother to give up this Jesse James fantasy and turn yourselves in."

"Jesse James fantasy?" Meg was in a towering rage. "Is that what this is to you? Our poor parents are in jail serving life sentences! You think anybody else is looking for evidence to prove they're innocent? You think the FBI is? Don't make me laugh!"

"Wait a second!" There was a note of surprise in the shock jock's usual bluster. "Are you saying that the only reason you and your brother are on the run is because you're trying to exonerate your parents?"

"Our parents were framed by a man named Frank Lindenauer! And we've already found out more about the guy than the FBI did during the whole trial. But nobody cares that they were supposed to be innocent until proven guilty! They just wanted someone to blame! And now it's done and forgotten, and our lives are *ruined*." Her voice cracked and she fell silent, gasping into the receiver in her effort to hold back sobs.

"Meg?" the famous voice prompted breathlessly. "Are you still there?"

Meg didn't answer. She couldn't. She was losing it, tearing up fast. Living this life, minute to minute, you were too busy surviving to see the big picture. But to take stock of it all — everything that had happened to their parents and themselves —

It was just so — so *sad*!

And I refuse to give this Big Mouth the satisfaction of hearing me cry!

With immense effort, she swallowed the bowling ball in her throat and steadied her voice. "So yeah, we'll turn ourselves in. But only when we've got enough evidence to overturn the conviction and get Mom and Dad out of prison. After that, if the police want to charge us for all the bad stuff we had to do to save our family, then I say it's worth it."

Her expression was not visible over the radio. Yet eleven million listeners and the Mouth himself had no trouble picturing the tough, righteous determination on the face of a heartbroken young girl. "That's how I see it," she said hoarsely. "You got a problem with that?"

She slammed down the pay phone and slumped against the wall, completely spent.

Had she remained on the line a moment longer, she would have heard something very rare on the Mouth of America Show: the legendary shock jock at a complete loss for words.

9

The Harley tooled along Federal Avenue past strip malls and subdivisions. Aiden drove slowly and carefully in the light traffic, resisting the bike's natural impulse to fly. Now, with HORUS Global Group's former headquarters just a few miles up the road, was no time to risk getting pulled over.

Denver Executive Center North looked like aliens had dropped a huge mirrored cube in the middle of a sprawling suburban neighborhood — an ultramodern twelve-story office building in a place where the next tallest features were trees.

They parked the motorcycle where it was hidden by much larger vehicles and walked to the main entrance. When the automatic doors slid shut behind them, both were confident that they had attracted little attention.

They were mistaken.

In a corner of the parking lot, a burly man sat in a

gold Corvette Stingray, watching them disappear in-side. If not for the Colorado Rockies baseball cap covering his completely bald head, the Falconers would have recognized him in a heartbeat.

This was the man Aiden and Meg called Hairless Joe. He had been pursuing them for thousands of miles, but he was no policeman or juvenile correc-tions officer. He had already tried to kill them three times.

Today he aimed to finish the job once and for all.

Dressed in the tan coveralls of the maintenance staff, he got out of the car and entered the lobby. He'd always known they would be coming here sooner or later. This plan had been in his mind ever since the Falconers had eluded him in California.

Normally, a gun was his weapon of choice — simple, quick, and deadly. But he couldn't risk that here — not so close to HORUS's former home.

This time it had to look like an accident.

Aiden and Meg stepped out of the elevator into a long hallway of medical and legal offices. Each prac-tice had its name stenciled into the frosted glass win-dow in the door.

Suite 1108 was blank.

"I thought it would be, you know, bigger, fancier — something," Meg whispered.

"What did you expect?" asked Aiden. "A neon sign that says WELCOME TO TERROR CENTRAL?"

"No crime-scene tape," Meg observed. "Are you sure this is the right place?"

"One way to find out." Aiden tried the door. Locked.

Meg's eyes fell on a fire extinguisher mounted in a recessed enclosure on the wall. "We could break the window, reach in, and flip the lock."

Aiden looked around. The hall was empty, but a lot of people worked here. And it might get a whole lot more crowded at the sound of shattering glass.

On the other hand, we didn't beat the odds just to stand around staring at a closed door. . . .

"Let me try something first." Aiden took the charity flyer from his pocket, folded it for strength, and inserted the edge between the lock and the frame. There was a click, and the door swung wide.

"Mac Mulvey," Aiden explained. The detective hero was also an expert burglar.

Meg was not a fan of their father's writing. With a nervous groan, she followed her brother into the suite where their family's horrible fate had been sealed.

The man called Hairless Joe rode the elevator to the twelfth floor, one higher than HORUS headquarters. With practiced expertise, he inserted a lock pick into the keyhole at the bottom of the control panel. The elevator car lurched and stopped dead. It was now frozen in place.

He strode to the stairwell and walked down to eleven. He approached the left elevator — the stalled side. A foot-long section of crowbar was concealed in his tool belt. He used it to jimmy open the metal panels. Then, grunting with effort, he pushed the doors wide, revealing the darkness of the empty shaft.

It would be a very long fall to the basement. A fatal fall.

His next stop was the janitorial closet. He pulled out a heavy floor polisher. The machine roared to life, buffing the terrazzo with three rotating brushes. The assassin positioned himself outside suite 1108. He knew the Falconer kids were on the other side of the door, but he dared not go in after them. The feds had been in control of that office for more than a year now. Who knew what surveillance equipment they might have in place?

Besides, Aiden and Meg would have to come out sooner or later.

It would be the last thing those two ever did.

Aiden and Meg looked around the HORUS offices in dismay. Suite 1108 was practically empty. There was furniture — desks, chairs, filing cabinets. But the drawers were bare, the files cleaned out. Whoever had searched this place had done a very thorough job.

Meg's frustration bordered on frenzy. "How can there be *nothing*?" She pulled out a file drawer, feeling behind and underneath it for lost or forgotten papers.

Aiden tried to be reasonable. "We're not CSI, Meg. The FBI was here before us. They're professionals at this kind of thing."

She got down on all fours to search the bottom of the cabinet. "We can't walk out of here with zero!"

Her brother nodded glumly. The two had known every kind of misery and despair since the arrest of their parents. Only the fact that there was a next step — somewhere to go, a clue to search for — had kept them from giving in to the terrible fate that had befallen their family. Meg was right. Leaving empty-handed was simply not an option.

A sudden gust from outside rattled the window. Two pairs of eyes followed the buzzing sound. They saw it at the same time.

Something had been jammed between the frame and the sash.

Meg frowned. "What's that?"

Brow furrowed, Aiden opened the window and reached for the small object. At first he thought it might be chewing gum. But when he touched it, he realized it was a piece of thin paper, folded down to the size of a postage stamp. The space was too tight for him to get a grip on the wadded-up sheet, so he worked it back and forth with his finger. The instant it was loose, the rattling noise became much louder.

"Cheap window," he decided. "The only way to keep it quiet was to wedge something in there." He drew the paper inside the room. Heads together, they watched as his trembling hands carefully opened it.

It was faded and ink stained, but it seemed to be a carbon copy of some kind of government form. The date read 2003.

"What is it?" Meg asked breathlessly.

"I'm not sure," Aiden replied slowly. "But I think

it's a list of all their employees and their social security numbers."

She scanned the page. "Where's Frank Lindenauer?" she exclaimed in bitter disappointment. "He's not on it!"

"He works undercover, Meg. He wouldn't be on any list. Even Mom and Dad's lawyers couldn't track him down. But," he added with determination, "I'll bet one of these people knows who he really is — and where."

"Then let's get out of here," Meg urged. "There's nothing else to find in this dump."

Aiden folded the paper and added it to the cache of leads in his pocket. Meg opened the door and peered into the hall. "Coast is clear," she whispered. "Just some janitor polishing the floor."

They left the office and stepped around the coveralled man and his buffing machine.

Powerful arms grabbed both Falconers by their throats.

10

Aiden flailed his arms in an attempt to free himself, but the grip was too strong. In the course of the struggle, the janitor's baseball cap toppled off a clean-shaven head.

A subzero chill flooded every capillary in Aiden's body.

It was Hairless Joe — the mysterious bald assassin who'd been tracking them since Vermont. The cold professional killer who — for reasons they could not fathom — wanted them both dead.

"Hey!" Aiden began.

The pressure on his neck intensified, a paralyzing vise that squeezed the sound from his vocal chords and dimmed his vision around the edges. Meg tried to scream, but Hairless Joe silenced her with a tightened grip around her neck.

Dragging the Falconers, the assassin bulled toward the elevators at the end of the corridor. Aiden

gawked in horror at the open doors and the empti-
ness beyond them.

He's going to throw us down the elevator shaft!

Aiden pounded frantically at Hairless Joe's head
and shoulders. In response, the crushing clinch on
his throat grew tighter, until he began to wonder if
he might die of strangulation before he could be
thrown to his death.

Amazingly, the thought of dying wasn't nearly as
awful as the thought of failing — leaving Mom and
Dad in prison with no hope of ever getting out.

Desperately, he kicked at the coveralls, but in his
weakened state he could not slow the bald killer's
progress. He could see the shaft now, yawning dark
and deep before them. The bottom was invisible
from up here. It would probably remain so until just
before the impact that would extinguish their young
lives.

Hairless Joe reared back to fling them into space.

Meg wrenched her head free and sunk her teeth
into their attacker's hand until she felt bone and
tasted blood. Hairless Joe howled in agony, releasing
the siblings. She scrambled up and grabbed the only
weapon within reach — the floor polisher.

It was too heavy to lift, so she swung it in an arc

along the terrazzo. It clipped the assassin across the back of both ankles, knocking his legs out from under him. As he went down, the momentum of the blow pitched him face-first into the shaft.

It was a split-second impulse, as natural as breathing. Aiden's arm shot out, grabbed a fistful of coverall fabric, and yanked.

It made all the difference. Instead of falling forward into the abyss, Hairless Joe slammed into the elevator door frame and sprawled back onto the floor, dazed. As he struggled to his feet, ready to come at them again, Aiden whirled around, grabbed the fire extinguisher, and shot a stream of foam into the bald man's face. It stopped the assassin in his tracks. Bellowing with rage and pain, he tried to clear his eyes of the stinging chemicals.

Office doors opened all down the hall. Concerned faces peered out, investigating the disturbance. What they saw — two unruly juveniles attacking a hapless janitor — was quite different from the reality.

Aiden dropped the extinguisher, and the Falconers took off into the stairwell. They scrambled and stumbled down the steps, propelled as much by gravity as by the impulse to escape.

"Faster, Meg!" Aiden urged. He barely dared to

glance over his shoulder for fear he'd be greeted by the sight of Hairless Joe in furious pursuit.

They did not stop running until they reached the Harley in the parking lot.

As the big bike roared off, leaving Denver Executive Center North behind, a pair of angry chemical-reddened eyes watched from an eleventh-floor window.

Meg clung to her brother's midsection, holding on as if the motorcycle's tires were navigating a tightrope over boiling lava. There hadn't been much to cheer about in this horrible misadventure. The one bright spot had been the fact that they'd given Hairless Joe the slip in California.

Or so we thought!

Now he was back, and more vicious than ever.

Stopped at a light, with the thunder of the Harley down to a dull roar, she leaned into Aiden's helmet. "How do you think he found us?"

"We've seen his fake police badge," her brother called back. "He can probably get cop reports, maybe even monitor their radio."

"Yeah, but the police don't know we're here," she countered. "Besides, Hairless Joe had more info than just Denver. He had the right building and the right floor and the right office. He didn't *follow* us; he was *waiting* for us — like he read our minds."

The light changed, and Aiden pulled over to the side of the road to let the traffic pass. "It has to be HORUS," he concluded. "He must have figured out that we're following up on our parents' case."

"What else does he know about us?" she asked worriedly. "The more he knows, the more he can anticipate what we're going to do."

Aiden pivoted on the seat to face her. He looked exhausted, almost gray — which was pretty much what you'd expect from someone whose only rest in the past two days had been a half-hour catnap in a bathroom. "*We* can't even anticipate what we're going to do most of the time, Meg. How easy can it be for a stranger?" He shrugged wearily. "We'll be more careful."

Meg hesitated. It was an awful thing, but it needed to be said. "We wouldn't have to be more careful if you hadn't saved the guy's life in the elevator shaft."

"I thought of that," Aiden admitted. "It just kind of happened. It was almost a reflex to grab him."

"Three times we got away from Hairless Joe," Meg told him, "and three times he came after us again. You can't tell me we're not better off if that guy's dead."

Aiden was appalled. "*He's* the murderer, not us!"

"That doesn't mean you have to go out of your way to *rescue* him! Finding Frank Lindenauer is hard enough without having to worry about Hairless Joe!"

"I thought we were the good guys," Aiden said bitterly.

"Mom and Dad were the good guys, too," Meg pointed out. "And look where it got them."

That settled it for Aiden. Mom and Dad were all that mattered.

"You're right. If we get another chance, we'll —" His voice cracked. He couldn't speak the words — that they might willfully act to end the life of another person. Even a person who wanted them dead.

Meg understood his conflicted feelings. It was okay to escape from a prison farm because they never should have been there in the first place. It was okay to break the law to preserve their freedom because that was the only way to help their parents. It made perfect sense, but where did it end?

Would it ever be okay to kill?

11

Back at the Hillsdale branch library, Aiden and Meg huddled in front of the computer monitor. Free Internet access had been the deciding factor in returning there. It was the only way to research the people on HORUS's Social Security form.

Aiden typed the first name into the Google.com home page. The search engine coughed up thousands of hits. Aiden clicked on the first link.

It was a news story dated February 21 of the previous year.

SWEEPING ARRESTS MADE IN HORUS TERROR CASE

I was a normal sixth-grader then, Meg thought in wonder. It was hard to believe she'd ever had a regular life of school and homework and family. That old Meg Falconer had no way of knowing that just two weeks later — on March 7 — an FBI battering ram would reduce her front door to tooth-picks and her parents would be hauled away in handcuffs.

Aiden investigated the other links. A series of articles described the arrest, trial, and conviction of HORUS Global Group's president. He was currently serving his sentence in Leavenworth Prison.

"Try another guy," Meg suggested.

But this man was in jail as well, another part of the plot to funnel money to foreign terrorists. The Falconers worked their way down the Social Security form, receiving similar results. Police raids, court trials, jury verdicts. All the names on the list seemed to be mixed up in the conspiracy. Guilty . . . guilty . . . guilty . . .

Prison . . . prison . . . prison . . .

Meg frowned. "If these people are in jail, how are we going to talk to them? We weren't even allowed to visit our own parents."

"We couldn't do it, anyway. We're wanted fugitives. We wouldn't last five seconds in a prison before somebody identified us." He typed in the last name on the list: EDITH WILKINSON.

A handful of links appeared on the screen. The first was a news story from the *Denver Post*. It was dated just a few weeks before the FBI raid on HORUS Global.

GRANDMOTHER DIES IN AUTO ACCIDENT

DENVER: A local grandmother was swept to her death when her car crashed through the guardrail of the Galveston Street Bridge and quickly sank in the icy waters of the South Platte River. Edith Wilkinson, 61, a part-time secretary for the Denver-based HORUS Global Group, was pronounced dead on arrival at Denver General Hospital.

"She's dead!" Meg gasped in shock. "Just our luck!"

"It wasn't great luck for her, either," Aiden reminded her gently.

Meg flushed. "I didn't mean it *that* way. It's just that she was the only person we might have been able to talk to."

"Wait —" Aiden was reading ahead in the article.

The official cause of the accident has not yet been determined, but police suspect excessive speed and driver error. Mrs. Wilkinson is survived by her daughter, Mrs. Jessica DeSouza, a science teacher at Liberty High School in suburban Glendale.

Meg was confused. "The daughter wasn't the one who worked for HORUS. How can we trace Frank Lindenauer through her?"

"She might remember stuff her mother told her. A month after this accident, HORUS got raided by the FBI. Your own family working for terrorists — that's not the kind of thing you forget." Aiden took a deep breath. "Anyway, she's all we've got."

"And we know where to find her," Meg added. "Liberty High School in Glendale."

Aiden checked the clock. "It's after four. School's out. We'll have to wait till tomorrow."

"Tomorrow?" Meg was distraught. "Aren't you forgetting something? We have nowhere to live! This isn't the boonies where you can curl up in any haystack. We're homeless in a big city!"

"I've been thinking about that," Aiden told her. "What if we just stay here?"

"What — at the library?"

"Why not? Listen — when we slept in the bathrooms, nobody had a clue. We hide in there right before closing, lie low while they lock the place around us, and come out when everybody's gone. Then the whole library's ours until they open again tomorrow. Maybe there's an employee kitchen where we can snarf some food."

That did it for Meg. Neither Falconer had eaten since the pie-eating contest in Idaho. Twenty-four heart-pounding hours had passed since then. She was so famished she was ready to pass out.

"Count me in." They had certainly spent nights in worse places. They could use the downtime to prepare for their meeting with Mrs. Jessica DeSouza.

And pray she can help us.

12

Aiden perched on the toilet tank so his feet would not be visible under the stall door. He needn't have bothered. With the lights off, the windowless bathroom was as dark as deep space.

A toxic mixture of fear and boredom made the minutes drag. It was hard to be afraid of librarians after surviving Hairless Joe. But a bookshelver could dial 9-1-1 as easily as anybody else. A cough at the wrong time, a clearing of the throat within earshot of a nosy employee — discovery was always as close as that.

It seemed like forever since he and Meg had moved the Harley from the parking lot to a less noticeable spot on one of the side streets. That had been about five-fifteen. They'd ducked into the bathrooms right after that. With no watch, it was impossible to tell how long he'd been waiting.

He heard the creak of the heavy door, followed by footsteps. His heart skipped a beat.

The lights came on. After suffocating darkness, the effect was like a nuclear flash. It jolted Aiden into full panic mode.

What should I do? Hide? Run for it?

"So this is the men's room," came a familiar voice.

"Meg, you lunatic!" He burst from the stall and glared at his sister. "You nearly gave me a heart attack!"

"Everybody's gone," she reported.

Aiden was wary. "Are you sure?"

"Positive. We're the proud owners of one library — at least till morning."

Food was the first order of business. They found a staff room behind the checkout desk, but the refrigerator offered only a few ketchup packets and a half-empty carton of cream for the coffeepot. Two gulps each and it was gone. It didn't even begin to satisfy their ravening hunger.

"What kind of a rip-off kitchen is this?" Meg complained. "Don't librarians have stomachs?"

"They probably brown-bag it," Aiden decided. "Or use the snack machines."

"Maybe we can break into one of those." Meg riffled through a cutlery drawer and came up with a bread knife. "This ought to do the trick."

"Too risky," said Aiden. "A busted machine might tip them off that they've got uninvited guests. Let's check the circulation desk — see if anybody left a sandwich or something."

But the search yielded nothing except library card applications, employee bulletins, and notepads with Dewey decimal numbers scribbled on them.

All at once, Meg let out a gasp.

Aiden was at her side in an instant. "What?" He goggled.

In a cupboard next to the book return sat a plastic garbage pail labeled OVERDUE FINES. It was piled high with coins.

Meg hesitated. "Seems a little sleazy, doesn't it? Swiping change from a library."

"Money means survival," Aiden said somberly. "Survival means —"

"A chance to help Mom and Dad," Meg finished. "I'm convinced."

Dinner was a vending machine smorgasbord — candy bars, chips, pretzels, animal crackers, beef jerky, pop tarts, peanuts, cookies, and Gatorade. It wasn't exactly a balanced meal, but the hungry fugitives devoured it like starving sharks.

"It's a good thing Mom isn't here," Meg observed,

mouth crammed full. "You know how she is about 'plastic food.' I can hear her now."

" 'Some of those pretzels are older than you are!' " the two chorused.

Their cascade of laughter died quickly with the thought of where their mother really was right then — in a federal maximum-security prison in Florida.

"Anyway," Aiden added soberly, "she'd be happy we aren't starving. Unhealthy food is still healthier than none."

Meg carefully counted every penny they removed from the pail — $11.85. "We're going to pay this back," she promised. "You know, when Mom and Dad are free, and we've got our normal lives again."

Classic Meg. She could be so tough, yet sometimes she was so naive! She honestly envisioned a rosy future where the Falconers were able to make everything right again. Aiden was only four years older, but he was reasonably sure the world didn't work that way. Every hour they spent on the run, their list of crimes grew longer. Why, just tonight they'd tacked on more trespassing and burglary. Surely they had passed the point of no return, where apologizing and paying for the damage wasn't enough.

PUBLIC ENEMIES • 77

Even if we do get Mom and Dad out of jail, how can we be sure that we won't just be taking their places?

They were in the children's section, lying in the Book Nook, a miniature castle made of beanbag-chair material. The sun had gone down, so the library was dark. They didn't dare turn on a light.

Aiden dreaded these moments — the thinking moments — almost as much as the fleeing and the fighting and the fear.

Now there was nothing to do *but* think — about the mess they were in; about Mom and Dad enduring the horrors of prison. About Hairless Joe and Emmanuel Harris, the J. Edgar Giraffe of their nightmares — the towering, coffee-guzzling FBI agent who had arrested their parents and had set his sights on Aiden and Meg.

And Frank Lindenauer, the worst of a bad bunch. The man who had destroyed John and Louise Falconer while pretending to be their friend.

Did Aiden and Meg really stand a chance of tracking down this terrible traitor and forcing him to admit what he'd done? They'd come so far, battled so hard, yet that goal still seemed a million miles away.

The feeling that came next made Aiden's stomach twist. It sickened him, yet he could not keep his mind from visiting that dark place, home to his greatest, deepest fear — the one he dared not speak aloud, even to Meg.

If they *did* find Frank Lindenauer, if the real truth was revealed . . . what if it turned out that Doctors John and Louise Falconer *hadn't* been framed? What if Mom and Dad had been guilty all along?

No! Aiden raged at himself. *Stop thinking that way! Shut down your brain!*

Beside him in the Book Nook, Meg had already begun to snore.

Aiden tossed and turned.

Federal Bureau of Investigation, Portland, Oregon.

Agent Harris could not take his eyes off the screen. The videotape, beamed over a secure network, showed Aiden and Margaret Falconer searching HORUS Global Group's former headquarters . . . in Denver.

Denver! With their pictures on the cover of every newspaper and a manhunt for them in four states, they had popped up twelve hundred miles away.

Those kids were something else!

"So they were in Denver when the girl placed the call to the radio show," Harris concluded.

"Definitely," the Portland supervisor replied. "There's less than an hour between the call to the Mouth of America and the kids' appearance on the surveillance camera. The show won't talk to us, though. They claim they're protecting their guests' privacy rights."

"I know." Harris had spoken to the Mouth personally to ask permission to put a trace on the station's phone line just in case the Falconers called in again. The shock jock had bluntly refused, even under threat of a court order. This was the kind of showboat who wasn't afraid of getting in trouble. He probably craved it. It was free publicity for his obnoxious show.

"Why didn't the Denver office pick the kids up?" asked Harris.

"It was too late. That camera isn't monitored full-time. It was pure coincidence that somebody scanned the tape last night. Lucky break for us, huh? Two fugitives just waltz into an office that's under federal surveillance?"

"Luck had nothing to do with it," said Harris. "They want to prove their parents are innocent. HORUS was a reasonable place to go."

The supervisor was flabbergasted. "Innocent? The Falconers? That was the biggest treason case in fifty years! You think we got it wrong?"

Harris clung to his Starbucks hot-cup. It was a question that kept him up nights — that and too much caffeine. "I don't know what to think anymore. But if this is my mess-up, whatever happens to those kids is my fault."

"Come on," chided the Portland man. "We're the FBI, not the Keystone Kops. We don't make mistakes on a case this important. Look" — he pointed to the screen, where Aiden and Meg were still combing the office — "you think those little punks are going to find so much as a crumb in there? Our people swept the place, and we didn't miss anything."

Both agents watched, transfixed, as Aiden pulled the wadded-up paper out of the window frame.

Harris started for the door. "Call Washington. I need everything we've got on the Falconer affair. Have them fax it to me ASAP."

"Here in Portland?" called the supervisor.

"No, in Denver. I'm going to get those kids."

13

Meg heard the *thump*, sat bolt upright, and got a faceful of plush castle.

What the —

Then she remembered. The Book Nook.

A shaft of harsh sunlight assailed her bleary eyes. Morning! Head in a fog, she searched the walls for a clock.

Eight-thirty. *Oh, no! The library opens at nine!*

Another *thump*. She peered out the window. Car doors! The staff was already arriving for the day!

She shook her brother. "Aiden, get up!"

He rolled over. "Wha —"

"We overslept! We've got to get back to the bathrooms! *Now!*"

One advantage of life on the run was that the Falconers had learned to go from deep sleep to frenzied action in the blink of an eye. They were out of the Book Nook, sprinting through the periodical section, when they heard the key in the lock.

Meg came to a stop so suddenly that Aiden ran into her from behind. The bathrooms were thirty feet away, but for them it might as well have been thirty miles. To get there, the fugitives would have to cross the glass entrance of the library — five feet in front of the employee at the door.

The door swung open, and in stepped a young man in a tweed jacket. Aiden and Meg stood frozen as he began switching on lights. Never before had they been trapped in a place with absolutely zero cover, without so much as a potted plant to hide behind or a shadow to lurk in.

The new arrival set down a briefcase, a newspaper, and a carton full of books. Meg calculated their chances of escape. *If we bolt, will he grab us? Or will he be so surprised . . .*

The man turned. In half a second, he'd be looking right at them.

Run —

Just as Meg was about to fly, dragging her brother behind him, the man walked back out to his car.

It was the kind of luck Aiden and Meg knew not to waste. They blasted past the entrance and disappeared into the bathrooms.

In a stall, perched on the toilet tank, Meg had to

press down with both feet to keep the trembling of her legs from rattling the seat.

It took twenty minutes for the machine-gun beating of Aiden's heart to return to normal. Every time someone entered the bathroom, he practically jumped out of his skin.

Calm down, he tried to soothe himself. *This is what you've been waiting for. The sooner the library is reasonably crowded, the sooner you can get out of here without attracting attention.*

He heard the door open with its characteristic squeak. Two men entered in mid-conversation.

". . . I don't know what takes more guts — running from the FBI or going toe-to-toe with the Mouth of America."

"Look who you're admiring," the second man commented. "She's an outlaw; her brother, too! They're probably both traitors, same as the parents."

"According to the girl, the parents are innocent."

"Yeah, and so was Al Capone. Some kid calls up the Mouth and says she's right and the entire United States government is wrong. Get real."

"I don't know. She was pretty convincing on the radio."

Seated on the toilet tank in his stall, Aiden couldn't believe his ears. *Meg — on the radio? On the Mouth of America show?*

He waited for the two men to exit the washroom, then slipped back into the library. The building was buzzing with families arriving for story hour, so he attracted no attention.

Meg was already at a computer station, printing MapQuest directions to Liberty High School.

Aiden took the seat beside her. "Tell me it isn't true. Tell me that, after weeks of breaking our necks to disappear, you didn't call a radio show with millions of listeners who are just as crazy as the nut job behind the mike."

Meg was shamefaced. "How'd you find out?"

"You *did*! How could you be so stupid?"

"It wasn't my fault," she said sheepishly. "He was saying all these rotten things about us."

"Who cares what the Mouth says?" Aiden hissed. "If we had a nickel for every time somebody insulted our family, we'd be the richest people on the face of the earth!"

Meg studied her hands on the keyboard. "I'm sorry," she mumbled. "You were sleeping. I do crazy things when you're not around."

"Oh, I get it. It's *my* fault." Aiden was bitter. "I hope you had the brains to keep your mouth shut about where we are."

"Of course. I didn't give up any information. I just thought I could make some points for Mom and Dad."

"And did you?"

She looked chagrined. "Nobody makes points with that jerk. It was a big mistake. Don't worry, I learned my lesson."

Aiden took a deep breath. "We've got enough problems with the cops and Hairless Joe after us, not to mention anybody who wants that reward. We can't afford to stir up the pot."

Meg pulled the directions out of the printer. "It won't happen again," she promised. "Now what's the plan for Mrs. Jessica DeSouza?"

The Falconers had already decided it would be unwise to reveal their true identity to the teacher from Glendale. It wasn't just the risk of being sold out for the reward money. Even a well-meaning adult might think that turning them in was the right thing to do.

"We stand a greater chance of being recognized if we're together," Aiden reasoned, "so I'll talk to her myself. A high school's a pretty big place. She probably doesn't know all the students. I can pass as one of them."

"You can pretend to be doing a project on terrorism," Meg suggested. "Here, I'll print that article about her mother's accident. You did an Internet search on HORUS, okay? And you saw her name. . . ."

Aiden listened carefully. No one had the gift of gab like Meg. She had talked them out of some very tough spots in the past.

En route to Glendale on the Harley, they stopped at a Mobil station to sink four dollars of the library's fine money into gas. The attendant seemed a little miffed at being paid in change, but otherwise he didn't seem suspicious.

Liberty High was a sprawling suburban campus — a good sign, Aiden decided. The bigger the school, the easier it would be to blend in. He left Meg in the parking lot with the bike and headed for the main entrance.

Funny, the instant he set foot inside the building, he felt so *normal*. After all, a high school student was what he was, what he *should* have been. The students bustling around, complaining about parents, homework, bad dates — he would have given any-

thing to have their ordinary lives and ordinary problems.

In the office, he met a secretary's eyes. "I'm supposed to see Mrs. DeSouza," he announced tenta-
tively.

The reply came in the exasperated tone of someone who had been asked far too many questions that
day. "Try the chemistry lab." And when Aiden
didn't immediately rush off, she added, "Upstairs,
straight down the hall."

Mrs. DeSouza was setting up experiment work
stations around an empty science classroom, stalking
from table to table, her lab coat billowing behind her
like a vampire's cape. Aiden stepped inside, and the
white cotton billowed in his direction.

"What can I do for you? We're going to be cen-
trifuging here next period."

Suddenly, Meg's coaching deserted him, and
Aiden went blank. He took the article out of
his pocket, unfolded it, and handed it to the
teacher.

Her features softened into an expression of sad-
ness as she recognized the story of her mother's fatal
accident. "Why did you bring this to me?" she asked
finally.

Aiden found his voice at last. "I'm writing a history paper on how terrorists get their funding. I was researching HORUS, and —"

He fell silent. It hadn't occurred to him that was probably a painful memory to ask Mrs. DeSouza to relive. *For Mom and Dad*, he reminded himself, forging on. "And when I found out you work at our school, I thought — "

"Mother wasn't mixed up in any of that," Mrs. DeSouza said insistently. "She was just the secretary — word processing, answering phones, that sort of thing. You could have knocked me over with a feather when I opened the paper and saw what those terrible people were up to. Of course, Mother was already gone by then."

"I guess her accident was a pretty big shock," Aiden offered lamely.

She nodded and sniffled. "And the craziest part is the police kept saying she must have been speeding, but Mother was the most cautious driver you've ever seen."

Aiden's brow furrowed. "So you don't believe the police report?"

Mrs. DeSouza shrugged wanly. "My believing or not believing isn't going to bring back the dead. My guess is that another driver lost control on that bridge, and Mother went through the railing trying to avoid him. One eyewitness mentioned a bald man racing away from the scene. But the police were never able to track him down."

Aiden froze.

A bald man . . . Hairless Joe?

What would a professional killer want with a sixty-one-year-old grandmother?

14

The pieces clicked into place. The "accident" had been no accident at all! Edith Wilkinson had been murdered, forced off the bridge by Hairless Joe.

But why?

The answer had to be HORUS. She must have stumbled upon what her employers were really involved in.

Now Aiden and Meg were the ones who were treading perilously close to the real truth.

That's why Hairless Joe is after us — he's a HORUS assassin!

"Mrs. DeSouza, did your mother ever talk about the people she worked with? Did she have any friends at HORUS?"

Mrs. DeSouza shook her head. "What could Mother have had in common with people like that? Terrorists — their sponsors, anyway. The scandal stretched all the way to those awful Falconers!"

Painfully, Aiden closed his ears and mind to the slur against his parents. This woman mustn't know how much her words stung him. "There had to be somebody," he persisted. "Someone she had lunch with or car-pooled with. Someone who gave her a lift when her car was in the shop?"

"Now that you mention it, there was one person," Mrs. DeSouza offered. "They weren't friends, exactly. But I know she felt sorry for this strange little man who swept up and did odd jobs around the office. Mother said he was a bit slow, but it must have been much more than that. He couldn't really speak. He seemed to be saying things without making any sense. And yet he and Mother always seemed to understand each other." She sighed. "My mother was a very kind person."

"Do you remember his name?" Aiden asked eagerly.

"All I know is that everyone called him Oznot. But I can't tell you if it's a first name, a last name, or a nickname. He couldn't have been part of the conspiracy. His mind wouldn't have been capable of it."

"Thanks, Mrs. DeSouza." Aiden was already backing out the door.

"Thank you," she said with a quiet smile.

"It's nice to know my mother isn't completely forgotten."

"Whoa, check out this tight ride!"

Meg was in the parking lot, hidden between a cargo van and an SUV, when the voice made her jump. Three tough-looking teenage boys were admiring the Harley, which was parked a couple of rows away. She crouched low, peering over the hood of the van as they twisted the throttle, squeezed the hand brake, and messed with the choke.

"This Eddie Staunton's bike?"

"Eddie Staunton rides a moped, genius. This is a top-of-the-line Harley."

Meg hung back, watching them poke and prod the machine. But when one of the teens climbed onto the saddle and began jumping on the kick start, she burst out of her cover. "Stop that!"

The three regarded her as if she were a mildly annoying insect.

"What's it to you?" asked the boy on the Harley.

"Get off my property," Meg demanded.

He hooted with derision. "*Your* property?"

Meg thought fast. She obviously couldn't be the owner of the motorcycle. But whose could she say it was? Her brother's? Too close to the truth. Her boyfriend's? They'd never believe it.

"It's my dad's."

"Your dad's in high school?" sneered one of the others. "What, did he flunk twenty years straight?"

Aiden stormed onto the scene. "What's going on?"

The three teens burst out laughing, jeering, "Hi, Dad!" and "You've got a lovely daughter, sir!"

All at once, the boy on the bike exclaimed, "Wait! I know you! You're those kids — the fugitives!"

"I don't know what you're talking about," Aiden said stiffly.

"The Falconers!" He scrambled off the Harley and stared at Aiden in awed respect. "The whole world's looking for you, man! You're famous!"

"What are you talking about?" scoffed one of the other teens. "It's not them. What would they be doing in this stupid place?"

Aiden got on the bike, and Meg took her place behind him. "You've got us mixed up with two other people," she insisted.

"No way!" The first boy stepped out in front of them. "I saw your pictures on CNN! You burned down a prison farm and stole cars. You stole this bike! All those cops, and you beat 'em! Can I shake your hands?"

In answer, Aiden started up the Harley and rolled the throttle, brushing the teen back and accelerating out of the parking lot.

Noon found the motorcycle parked outside a small Internet café in a downtown neighborhood far from Liberty High School.

Aiden and Meg hunched over a computer monitor. The Internet access and the dollar-store baseball caps pulled down to hide their all-too-recognizable faces had left them nearly broke. Of the money they had taken from the bucket of overdue fines, a grand total of fifteen cents remained.

The Google search had not gone well. "There's no Oznot in Denver," he grumbled. "There's no Oznot anywhere."

"Maybe you spelled it wrong," Meg suggested.

"I spelled it with a *Z*, an *S*, even an *AU*. Nothing. It's not a real name."

"Must be his nickname," she concluded.

"That won't help us find him, Meg."

A woman sat down at a nearby table, lost in the depths of a tabloid newspaper. Aiden was so distracted and discouraged that he read the banner headline several times before its meaning registered.

MOUTH TO COPS: "LEAVE FALCONER KIDS ALONE!"
SHOCK JOCK TALKS OF LITTLE ELSE SINCE MARGARET
FALCONER'S DRAMATIC CALL

Aiden tapped Meg on the shoulder and directed her attention to the headline.

Meg gawked. "Leave us alone?" she whispered. "That's not how it was at all! He hates our guts! He wants us in jail!"

Aiden took her arm and led her out of the café. "This is serious, Meg. We were always kind of well known because of Mom and Dad, but we're getting way too famous." He looked nervously from face to face in the passing parade of pedestrians. Which of these people would be the one to point or shout or dial 9-1-1 on a cell phone? He steered her into an alley. "I mean, how are we supposed to find Frank Lindenauer if we can't even go out in public without being recognized?"

"Maybe it's not as bad as it looks," Meg offered. "Okay, the Mouth has a thing for our family, but he's too much of a windbag to obsess on any one subject for long."

Aiden set his jaw. "We can't be sure of that. We have to listen for ourselves and hear what that guy is saying about us."

That meant finding a store that sold radios, or at least had one tuned to the Mouth of America show. As a safety precaution, they walked half a block away from each other, the brims of their hats pulled down low.

McMichael's Small Appliances was a small show-room that specialized in vacuum cleaners, but there was a display of radios tucked away in a corner al-cove. Aiden and Meg entered separately and met up there.

Aiden fiddled with the tuner on a display model until he heard the despised voice. Just the sound of it triggered terrible memories. During their parents' trial, the Mouth of America had urged his listeners to write to the judge, calling for John and Louise Falconer to die in the electric chair. More than two hundred thousand had actually done it. The shock jock's fans were more like his army, ready to follow him to the ends of the earth.

"Look, I talk to a lot of people," the Mouth was ranting. "I know a snow job when I hear one. Meg Falconer is telling the truth — I'd bet my life on it!"

"But you yourself said she and her brother are criminals," the caller pointed out.

"Yeah, and who made them criminals? We did! You take two kids and turn them into hunted animals — of course they'll do whatever it takes to stay free! As for the parents — maybe they're innocent. Meg says she and her brother have found new evidence. Hey, it wouldn't be the first time the government railroaded somebody just to close a case. That's how I see it! You got a problem with that?"

Aiden and Meg exchanged bewildered glances. How had the Mouth suddenly become their ally? What had prompted this astonishing change of heart?

"You're turning into one of those bleeding hearts you hate so much," the caller accused.

"At least I *have* a heart," the Mouth snapped back. "Meg — if you're out there — I'm on your side. Call again. There must be some way I can help you and your brother. I'm a powerful guy — I've got millions of listeners all over the country. People care about what I say. If there's anything I can do for you — *anything* — you just have to ask!"

Aiden switched off the radio, and the Falconers regarded each other in amazement.

"Well," mused Aiden, "I don't know what you said on that guy's show yesterday, but it must have been the right thing."

"Do you think it's a trap?" Meg asked suspiciously. "You know, like the FBI has a trace on his line?"

"He sounds sincere. Then again, he also sounded sincere when he was trying to get Mom and Dad executed."

She was blown away. "Should I call?"

"Absolutely not. What good could it do? It's not like the Mouth can issue a presidential pardon. He's a talk show host — an opinionated jerk who gets paid for being an opinionated jerk on the radio. It would just make us even more notorious, which would make it that much harder for us to help Mom and Dad."

Meg regarded him in despair. The odds had always been stacked against them. But now there was a new element — a ticking clock.

We've got to find Frank Lindenauer before we're so famous that it's impossible to stay free.

Agent Harris's first stop was Denver Executive Center North, eleventh floor.

"Juvenile delinquents, that's who it was!" exclaimed the elderly eyewitness who worked as receptionist for the chiropractor in suite 1117. "I heard a commotion, and when I looked out, there they were — two young roughnecks, manhandling the elevator repairman!"

The FBI man held up a copy of the cell-phone photo. "Were these the kids?"

"That's them!" the woman exclaimed in surprise. "The smaller one couldn't have been more than ten or eleven." She squinted at the picture. "Is it a boy or a girl?"

Harris didn't answer. He knew that Margaret Falconer had cut her long hair short soon after the escape from Sunnydale Farm. From a distance, she was often mistaken for a boy.

"Any idea where I can find the repairman?" asked Harris. "Does he work for the building?"

The woman shook her head. "He wasn't one of their usual men. In fact, I haven't seen him before or since. I suspect he was fired. His safety record is almost criminal. He left the elevator doors wide open to the shaft! That has to be a code violation."

Harris frowned. "Describe him."

The receptionist peered up at the six-foot-seven agent. "You'd probably call him short, but I remember him as quite tall. And big — stocky. I was surprised kids would tangle with him. He was wearing coveralls. And, oh, yes — he had a large head, shaved completely bald."

Ice-cold understanding came to Emmanuel Harris. It was *him* — the mysterious assassin the Falconers called Hairless Joe.

He thought of the elevator shaft — a deadly fall to the basement far below. This was no fight. It was another homicide attempt — the latest of several since the killer had begun his pursuit of the Falconers in Vermont.

That was why Harris had never released to the press that Aiden and Margaret were in Denver. He'd been afraid to risk providing the mysterious killer with a clue that might enable him to finish his gruesome task.

Yet Hairless Joe had found them anyway. He must have known of the HORUS connection. What could that mean?

Whatever the answer to that question, it was not as urgent as the search for the Falconers themselves. Police custody was the only safe place for them now.

Just yesterday they had narrowly escaped a horrible death in the basement of this building.

Next time they might not be so lucky.

Meg bent over the wastebasket of coins, stuffing fistfuls of change into her burgeoning pockets. They had returned to the Hillsdale branch because they had nowhere else to go — no place to sleep, no money for food, and worst of all, no lead to follow.

Living on stolen overdue fines, she reflected glumly. *Surely we've hit rock bottom.* She cast an irritated look at her brother, who was building neat stacks of quarters, dimes, nickels, and pennies.

"What are you doing?"

"Maximizing buying power," he explained reasonably. "Quarters are worth the most, but dimes take up less pocket space . . ." His voice trailed off.

Typical Aiden. Even in a spot like this, he had to be an efficiency expert.

They shared another dinner of vending-machine junk food. Mom probably would have had a heart attack.

It has to be better than the food where she is now —

No. Meg had promised herself not to think about their parents in prison. It was just too awful. Mom and Dad locked away. Aiden and Meg outlaws, renegades. Their quest to save the family stalled . . .

All because there's no such name as —

And suddenly, there it was, gazing down at her from the wall — the clue that had stopped them in their tracks, the five letters that were tormenting them — *Oznot.*

The Hillsdale branch was decorated with photographic prints of old Denver. Behind the circulation desk, not five feet away, was a sepia-tone picture of a city street, with antique automobiles clogging the roadway. A billboard proclaimed BUY WAR BONDS. World War II, probably — the cars appeared to be from the nineteen forties. On one corner was a restaurant, its name spelled out in lights: OZNOT'S DELICATESSEN.

"Aiden — look!"

He frowned at the framed photo. "Why didn't that come up on any of our searches?"

Meg shrugged. "The place might have closed decades ago."

"Like a family business. The parents retire, and the kids don't want to run it anymore. But that still doesn't explain why there are no Oznots in the phone book."

"Maybe they changed their name," Meg suggested. "I would have."

"Or maybe the Oznot at HORUS was the last of the family. Mrs. DeSouza said he had some kind of mental handicap. They probably had to shut down the restaurant because he wouldn't have been able to keep it going. And if he can't communicate, what would he need with a phone?"

Meg nodded. "It makes sense. But that still doesn't help us find the guy."

Aiden leaned over the counter, scrutinizing the sharp black-and-white image. "Check it out — you can read the street signs. That's definitely an eight. Eighth and — could it be Myers? It starts with *M-Y*."

They consulted the wall map in the reference section. Sure enough, Eighth Avenue intersected Myerson Place just east of downtown.

Meg was confused. "So we know where the restaurant used to be. So what?"

"We can talk to the locals, maybe find some old-timer who remembers the place and the family who ran it." Aiden took a deep breath. "It isn't much, but it's all we've got to go on right now."

Meg nodded uneasily. This sliver of a lead, this mixture of clue, hunch, and wild guess, was the only thing keeping their quest alive.

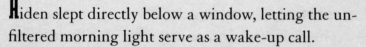

16

Aiden slept directly below a window, letting the unfiltered morning light serve as a wake-up call.

Another ticking clock, he thought as he hid in the bathroom, waiting for the staff to open up the Hillsdale branch. All around him, time seemed to be running out. How much longer could they live in the library before somebody noticed the kids who were always there first thing in the morning and right before the library closed?

And the Harley — that was another time-limited offer. Sooner or later, the out-of-state license plate would attract attention.

For the moment, though, his fears proved to be unfounded. He and Meg left the library without incident, and the motorcycle was exactly where they'd left it, surrounded by parked cars, not undercover police officers.

He felt almost human again as he merged the

Harley onto I-25 South. For a fugitive, two nights in a row of real sleep was a rare luxury.

After twenty minutes, they exited the highway into a canyon of skyscrapers and stadiums, past the state capitol into a neighborhood of lower, flatter structures.

"Keep an eye out for Myerson Place!" he called over his shoulder to Meg.

The command was unnecessary. For there, coming up on the right, was the building that had once housed the old delicatessen. It was a one-hour photo developing shop now, yet it was unmistakable — the same display window, the same ornate front door. They could even see where the lights had once spelled out *Oznot's*, shadowed in flowing script across the stucco facade.

They parked the Harley in a back alley and walked out to the street. "Wait here," Aiden advised. "I'll see if the photo guy remembers the delicatessen."

The photo store was a one-man operation with a darkroom at the back and a developing machine along the side. It was spitting out snapshots of Disney World as Aiden approached the counter.

The clerk looked up from an envelope he was preparing. "What can I do for you, son?"

"I'm not sure," Aiden said. "Didn't this used to be a restaurant called Oznot's?"

"Yeah." The man smiled. "When you were about three. What's the big interest?"

"My dad always talked about the corned beef in this place."

"Well, we don't have any," the clerk told him. "Lots of film, no corned beef."

"Did you take over when the deli went out of business?" Aiden forged on.

"Oh, sure. Right after the vet, the pizza parlor, the guitar shop, and Congressman Stevenson's campaign headquarters." He jerked his thumb in the direction of the entrance. "What's up with your friend?"

Aiden turned to the door. His sister was jumping and waving, doing everything except sending up signal flares to attract his attention.

Hastily, he apologized to the man and ran outside. "Is this how you keep a low profile?"

She cut him off. "Didn't Mrs. DeSouza call Oznot a strange little guy?" she whispered.

"I think so. Why?"

She dragged him around the corner onto Myerson Place, where they could see the side of the wood-shingled building. The jagged line of a fire escape decorated the rearmost windows. On the second floor, holding a watering can over a collection of potted plants on the iron landing, was one of the oddest-looking people Aiden had ever seen. His head was enormous. Yet on second glance Aiden realized that the head was normal-sized — it was the shoulders and upper body that were tiny, giving the young man the appearance of an alien. He was tending his plants with intense concentration, like a doctor performing microsurgery.

"Can it be this easy?" Meg whispered.

Over the past weeks, every centimeter of progress had come only at the expense of blood, sweat, and stomach lining. For the object of their search to be hanging out a window seemed awfully convenient.

Yet it made sense. "Maybe the Oznot family still owns the building," Aiden guessed. "They can't kick him out if he's the landlord."

The entrance to the apartments was a locked stairwell next to the photo place. The buzzers were unmarked, so Aiden tried the bell next to the number two. There was no actual reply, but they heard a soft click, followed by tinny breathing from the intercom speaker.

Aiden cleared his throat. "Mr. Oznot?"

The battered wooden door buzzed open.

The stairs were ancient and dusty, creaking with every step.

Meg shot her brother a dubious look. "This is great — we survived everything under the sun so we could walk right into the apartment of a maniac."

"Grandmothers don't hang out with maniacs," Aiden argued, as much to reassure himself as his sister.

Oznot was in the doorway waiting for them. Backlit by the bright apartment in the dim hall, he resembled a stick figure — long, skinny arms and legs, rail-thin body supporting a substantial round head. He seemed genuinely thrilled to see them, although Aiden couldn't imagine why. Maybe he just liked company. He probably didn't get many visitors.

"Hi, Mr. Oznot," Aiden greeted. "Thanks for letting us in. I'm Gary Graham, and this is my friend Belinda." In the past few weeks, the Falconers had assumed so many identities that fake names rolled easily off the tongue. "We were hoping to talk to you about the place where you used to work — HORUS Global."

In response, he got a bright smile, followed by a series of syllables that sounded like conversation but were really gibberish. Both Aiden and Meg could only stand and stare.

A trifle frustrated, Oznot repeated his speech, sound for sound and tone for tone.

Meg was dumbfounded. "Another language?"

"I don't think so," Aiden replied in a low voice. "Mrs. De Souza said he just can't communicate."

"Then what are we doing here?"

"We'll make it work," Aiden insisted. "We've got no choice." To Oznot, he said, "We're interested in someone you used to work with. A man named Frank Lindenauer."

Oznot continued to talk in his strange meaningless way. His expression failed to reveal whether or not "Lindenauer" rang a bell with him. He might have been talking about the man who had framed their parents. But he just as likely might have been giving them his secret recipe for egg salad.

In a lightning motion, Meg reached into Aiden's pocket and pulled out the old photograph of "Uncle Frank" from that vacation long ago. She held it in front of their host, praying it would do the trick. "That's him."

A torrent of babble poured from Oznot. There

was no mistaking his message this time. He knew that face.

In a flurry of excitement, he hurried them into his shabby but neat living room and all but shoved them down on the worn couch. From a side table, he pulled a large art pad and began flipping through dozens of pencil drawings.

Meg was impressed. "This is *your* work?" The Falconers noted that the walls were hung with these black-and-white sketches, most of them portraits, all of them done with confident skill and remarkable attention to detail. As severe as his communication handicap may have been, Mr. Oznot was very much able to express himself through his art.

At last, their host came to the page he had been searching for and held it up for their inspection. It was a head-and-shoulders image of a man with long hair, mustache, and beard.

Frank Lindenauer.

There was no question about it. This was the same person as the one in the photograph. It was a remarkable likeness, right down to the quality of the skin and the bristly thickness of the facial hair. In a way, the sketch was even more complete because it was a close-up. They could see furrows in the forehead, crinkles at the corners of the eyes, even a slightly chipped front tooth in the smiling mouth.

"That's him!" Aiden exclaimed. "We need to find him! Do you know where he lives?"

From Oznot came the clearest message thus far — a helpless shrug.

"He doesn't know," Meg translated.

Aiden was grasping at straws. "Let's look through the pictures. There are HORUS people in there. Maybe we'll stumble on some kind of clue." He began turning pages, peering anxiously into each well-drawn face.

"It's no use," Meg said miserably. "We don't know anybody from HORUS. How would we recognize —"

The cry that erupted from both throats startled Oznot. The drawing was so unexpected and so terrifyingly lifelike that it was as if they had suddenly found the man himself in the living room.

It was a portrait of Hairless Joe.

17

The assassin's eyes were murderous and burning, his face hardened by fury to the point where his mouth was barely a thin line.

"You know *him*, too?" Meg demanded. "Who is he?"

Oznot became animated, speaking quickly, gesturing with both hands. He was obviously trying to tell them something, but what? What did he know about Hairless Joe? How much could Oznot, who only swept up at HORUS, know about the evil organization's secret assassin?

For the next hour, Aiden and Meg stayed with the strange little man, poring over his hundreds of drawings, desperately searching for some way to communicate with him. The one thing they understood from Oznot was how hard he was trying to get through to them and share what he knew.

"It's useless," Meg moaned. "He's a sweet guy, but we're never going to figure out what he's trying to say — if he's got anything to say at all. We can't be sure of that, either."

Reluctantly, Aiden agreed. In all these weeks on the run, the heartbreak, heroics, Herculean efforts, and narrow escapes, this was the most difficult decision they'd been forced to make — to abandon their only clue, thank Mr. Oznot for his help, and walk out of the apartment with no place to go from there.

They were halfway down the stairs when a series of yelps from Oznot stopped them in their tracks.

"Is he calling us?" Meg asked.

"It's useless," Aiden said despondently. "Even if he knows Frank Lindenauer's home address, how's he going to give it to us?"

But useless or not, the man caught up with them. In a state of agitation, he took each one by the wrist and hauled them back up to the apartment. He was working hard to get his message across — jabbering excitedly and pointing out the window at the cars below.

"It's okay, Mr. Oznot."

And then a glimmer of sunlight reflected off something inside a gold Corvette parked across the street. Aiden narrowed his focus. It wasn't metal or chrome or glass. It was skin — the smooth, shiny scalp of a completely bald head.

The driver of the Corvette was Hairless Joe.

A wheeze of terror confirmed that Meg had spotted him, too. They ducked down beneath the windowsill.

"How could he find us *here*?" she rasped.

"He's probably been keeping an eye on the place," Aiden replied. "Oznot's the only HORUS employee who's not either dead or in jail right now."

Oznot waved his sketchbook in their faces, open to the assassin's portrait.

"We *know*!" Aiden exclaimed impatiently. "Listen — is there another way out of here?"

Their host instantly understood. He hurried them to the rear of the apartment to the bedroom window, which led to the fire escape. It was perfect. While Hairless Joe was watching the front door on Eighth Avenue, they would be climbing down onto Myerson Place, away from his view.

Aiden swung a leg outside, careful not to step on the plants. He reached in and helped his sister onto the landing beside him.

"Thanks, Mr. Oznot," she whispered. She turned to Aiden. "Do you think he's in any danger? Remember, Hairless Joe killed Mrs. DeSouza's mother because she knew things about HORUS."

"If Hairless Joe was worried about Oznot, he

would have done something about it months ago," Aiden replied. "Oznot could never be a threat, because how could he testify in court? No one would understand him."

He yanked on the lever to lower the ladder to street level. With a screech and crash that sounded like an aircraft carrier ramming an iceberg, the ancient wrought-iron extension dropped into place. Frozen with shock and fear, the Falconers stood rooted to the fire escape. Surely that much noise would attract not just Hairless Joe but also every cop in Denver.

They waited, eyes riveted on the corner, ready to dive back into the apartment the instant their dangerous enemy came running into view.

Aiden counted to ten. Then twenty.

Nothing.

"Okay," he whispered.

They climbed down the ladder and jumped to the sidewalk.

Hairless Joe was less than fifty yards away. *I can't see him*, Aiden thought, *but he's there, deadly and waiting*.

With the assassin staking out the corner of Eighth and Myerson, the Falconers walked in the opposite direction to Seventh, circling back to the narrow alley where the Harley was parked. To complete the loop, they had to traverse twenty yards of Eighth Avenue, in full view of the Corvette.

Hairless Joe's attention was on Oznot's apartment, but —

If we can see him, he can see us.

Aiden forced his eyes down to the sidewalk and rounded the corner to the alley.

They sprinted for the Harley.

"Think he spotted us?" Meg panted, all but hurling herself onto the saddle.

Aiden took his place in front of her. "I'm not hanging around to find out!"

The bike roared to life, and they sped up the alley. Aiden rolled the throttle with one hand while shrugging into his helmet aided by the other. In a matter of seconds, they'd be on Eighth Avenue — a risky moment, sure. But then the Harley's big engine could rocket them far away from the man who wanted them dead.

Suddenly, a sleek shape squealed nimbly around the corner.

It was the gold Corvette — coming right at them!

18

Aiden felt his sister's shudder over the vibration of the motorcycle. They could see Hairless Joe's cold, determined features through the windshield. This time he was planning to use the car as his murder weapon. He was going to run them down.

Aiden veered left, hugging the wall in an attempt to sneak the bike past their less maneuverable attacker. Hairless Joe swerved directly into their path. Aiden tried the other side, getting so close that the bricks whizzed by barely an inch from the Harley's handlebar. The Corvette followed. Its passenger mirror struck a doorway and snapped off, but the assassin did not slow.

They were trapped — trapped in a dead-end alley.

How can I get past this guy?

Then he saw it — a sack of garbage that had toppled into the lane. It was ten feet from the car's front bumper.

"Hang on!" Aiden twisted the accelerator, and the bike leaped forward in a burst of raw power. They reached the trash bag a split second before Hairless Joe got there. The Harley's front wheel struck it and lurched onto the Corvette's hood. In a howl of torque, the motorcycle climbed the car like a ramp. The tire ricocheted off the windshield, cracking it.

Aiden looked down to see Hairless Joe behind the wheel, staring at them in utter disbelief. The image passed below, and they were airborne, sailing up and over the Corvette. Frantically, Aiden yanked back on the handlebars to avoid nose-diving into solid concrete. The Harley came down on its rear wheel, an impact they felt in their molars. They bounced twice before the front of the bike found the earth again. The tire bit into the pavement, and the machine rocketed out of the alley and wheeled onto Eighth Avenue.

Aiden checked his mirror. The Corvette's white reverse lights were on.

Meg was bug-eyed. "If I ever call you boring again," she shouted in his ear, "just remind me about today!"

He poured on the gas, weaving in and out of the slow-moving traffic. "It's not over yet! He's coming after us!"

Horns sounded and angry shouts rang out as the Corvette backed into the middle of Eighth Avenue. In a cloud of burning rubber, it took off in hot pursuit.

An ordinary car would have been no match for the Harley. But the gold roadster was hardly a pushover, built for speed with a four-hundred-horsepower engine. It was being driven by a stone-cold killer who probably had dozens of high-speed chases under his belt. Aiden was unlicensed and underage. Three days ago, he had never so much as sat on a motorcycle, much less driven one.

It would take a miracle to beat this guy, he thought grimly.

The Harley slalomed down Eighth Avenue, running lights.

"Faster!" Meg shouted. "He's gaining on us!"

A glance in the mirror confirmed that the Corvette was half a block behind and closing the gap.

Aiden leaned on the handlebars and wheeled the chopper around a sharp corner. The sports car skidded into the intersection but made the turn.

On this less crowded street, it was a drag race. The Falconers watched in horror as Hairless Joe drew even with them. Aiden could see the implacable expression on the face of their pursuer. It was more terrifying than malice or fury. It was pure ruthless efficiency, devoid of emotion.

The car inched sideways toward the Harley, crowding the bike off the roadway. The motorcycle's tires gained purchase on the gravel shoulder, spraying stones in all directions. Aiden's eyes mapped the course ahead. The shoulder continued for a few hundred yards and then disappeared into —

"A bridge!" Meg exclaimed.

Aiden had a horrifying vision of Edith Wilkinson's final moments — plunging into the South Platte River, run off a bridge by a bald man. He knew, deep in his marrow, that he and his sister would not leave that overpass alive.

Meg seemed to sense that something was about to happen. She put a death grip around her brother's midsection and tensed for action.

The span was twenty yards away. Then ten. Aiden waited until the last possible second and wrenched the bike off the road. They jounced down a steep embankment in a mini-avalanche of rocks and clumps of dirt. Plowing through tall weeds and underbrush at the edge of the road below, they climbed onto the pavement and took off.

"Nice one, bro!" Meg cheered.

Aiden let up on the throttle a little, slowing to the speed of traffic. Now that they'd lost Hairless Joe, it was time to blend in with the other vehicles.

The road took them farther from downtown, into a green, leafy suburb. As they crested a hill, the Harley's engine coughed once, and the machine lurched.

"What's that?" Meg shouted in alarm.

Aiden checked the fuel gauge. "We've got to stop for gas!"

"What — *now?*"

He scanned both sides of the road ahead for a service station. What he saw instead made his blood run cold. There, waiting at a light, was the gold Corvette.

"How'd he find us?" Aiden exclaimed aloud.

"Maybe he lives here," Meg suggested. "Knows the roads."

Suddenly, the sports car mounted the sidewalk, peeled around an SUV, and shot right out in front of them.

Frantically, Aiden leaned left so hard he thought the Harley would wipe out flat. He slid by the Corvette, missing the taillight by a hair. With a blast of its horn, a small Saturn, wheels locked, slammed into the Corvette, crumpling the trunk. Hairless Joe didn't even acknowledge the accident. He gunned the engine in pursuit of the speeding motorcycle.

Feeling the motorcycle buck again, Aiden swallowed a rising panic. *Chased by a killer, running out of gas — how could it be worse?*

The answer came in the form of a wailing siren.

19

A black-and-white police cruiser pulled out and joined the chase.

Meg stared over her shoulder in disbelief at the train of vehicles behind them — first the Corvette, then the police car.

The only bright spot was that the cop might keep Hairless Joe from murdering them.

But we'd be caught!

Meg couldn't see her brother's face; the tense muscles at the base of his neck told the story.

Up ahead, the light turned red, stopping a cluster of vehicles in front of them. Holding their breath and tucking in their elbows and knees, Aiden and Meg made themselves skinny and shot through the narrow opening between two sedans. They flashed directly into the path of an oncoming Denver city bus. With a roar, Aiden yanked the throttle and they hurtled past, a split second ahead of disaster.

Before the horrified eyes of onlookers, the gold Corvette drove up on the sidewalk, sending a wire mesh garbage can flying. Pedestrians dived for their lives as Hairless Joe sailed over the curb and followed the Harley right through the intersection.

The police cruiser squealed to a halt behind the line of stopped cars. The officer wisely decided not to put any more citizens at risk by continuing pursuit.

Instead, he reached for his radio.

It was more of a closet than an office, and it looked even smaller with the six-foot-seven Emmanuel Harris inside. FBI headquarters in Denver was overcrowded, and this little cubbyhole was the best they could manage. There was no room for a desk, so his chair was pulled over to a shelf. There he sat, buried in a mountain of paper, the FBI's complete file on *The People versus John and Louise Falconer* — the trial of the new millennium, the most famous treason case of the past fifty years.

He had promised those kids that their parents' convictions would be reviewed. Sure, they hadn't believed him, but he intended to keep his word.

A local agent stuck his head in the door. "Hey, Harris, thought you'd like to know — Denver PD just put out an APB on a gold Corvette chasing a Harley."

Harris jumped up, whacking his head on a dangling bare bulb. "Kids on the bike?"

The man nodded. "Idaho plates. Sounds like your Falconers."

When the two agents left the building, the Denver man was running to keep up with Harris's long, purposeful strides.

The Harley's fuel gauge was on dead empty now, and even the slightest upgrade caused the big engine to sputter. Hairless Joe was right on their tail, never more than a few yards back, waiting for the moment to strike.

Aiden scanned ahead in a desperate search for a place where the Harley would fit and the Corvette wouldn't. There was nothing — just houses, buildings, and small stores. Nowhere to run, nowhere to hide.

Meg pointed. "Look!"

At first, Aiden thought it was some kind of botanical garden — tall wrought-iron gates, dense with lush greenery. Then he caught a glimpse inside. It was a cemetery, lined with an endless pattern of close-ranked grave markers. A muted mosaic sign declared the place to be Centennial Acres.

Without hesitation, Aiden steered into the driveway. In a roar of four hundred horses, the Corvette followed. Aiden gritted his teeth. He felt bad for what he was about to do, but there was no way around it. It was their only chance to lose Hairless Joe.

He wheeled off the pavement and began to snake between tombstones, breathing silent apologies to the people whose graves his tires were trampling.

Meg gripped his arm from behind. "Oh, my God!"

The Corvette was navigating behind them, wide, spinning tires spraying turf and mangled flowers in all directions. The gold car twisted and bounced like an airboat in the Everglades. Scratching and denting itself on some tombstones, knocking others flat, it lurched forward, slowed but not stopped.

The Harley was the better off-road vehicle, but Hairless Joe was relentless and cared nothing for his car. Aiden kicked down into first gear in a desperate attempt for more speed as he searched the vast grounds for a spot too tight for the Corvette. It was working — the bike was beginning to open up a lead — when the engine sputtered, coughed, and died.

20

Aiden jumped on the kick start once, twice. The Harley was still, its fuel tank bone-dry. He tried again — three times, four —

Meg had to drag him off the motorcycle. "Forget the bike! Run!"

They fled, pounding down the rows of graves in a ghoulish footrace. The Corvette was upon them in seconds. Hairless Joe stepped on the gas, determined to finish his dirty job here and now.

It was the ultimate mismatch — two kids on foot versus a four-hundred-horsepower engine with a madman at the wheel. Aiden and Meg sprinted for their lives as the Corvette thundered up behind them.

As one person, the Falconers dived over a large double headstone at the end of a row. They hit the ground beyond it and rolled.

The Corvette slammed into the granite slab, hurtling metal against eternal stone. Stone won. The hood of the car flattened like an accordion. Hairless Joe disappeared behind the billowing white of an airbag.

Aiden and Meg got up and ran, making for an area of the cemetery where there were stands of trees and brush that would provide some cover.

"Think he's dead?" Meg panted.

"He's never dead!" her brother replied. "Keep moving!"

They could hear distant sirens all around. And — was that a helicopter overhead?

We've been so worried about Hairless Joe that we forgot the cops, Aiden realized with a shudder.

"We need a place to hide," he said. "Now!"

Nestled in a small grove of poplars stood the Schuyler family mausoleum, a white marble temple with a domed roof and pillars.

They made for it, bounding up the stone steps and slipping inside through the heavy door. The place was empty and oppressively silent. One wall was lined with elaborately carved niches. At least half of these were filled with a variety of sealed urns, identified by brass plaques.

Ashes, Aiden concluded. He wondered if he and his sister would be the next dead people in here.

"It's not as creepy as I thought," Meg observed,

and then dropped her voice to a whisper when she realized how sound echoed in the stone chamber. "I expected spiderwebs and bats and stuff."

"The family probably pays someone to look after the place," Aiden whispered back. "Believe me, it's plenty creepy!"

In an instant, all thoughts of the mausoleum and its dead were wiped from their minds with the sound of a single footstep on the stairs outside.

In a rush of shock and fright, Aiden scanned the room. There was no escape and no cover.

He had always known that the odds were stacked against them. Yet this seemed like a particularly unpleasant place for it all to end.

Mom, Dad — we tried —

When the heavy door began to move, he pushed Meg into a shadowed corner in a pathetic attempt to protect her.

He saw the bald head silhouetted against the bright sunlight outside. Aiden raised his arms to defend himself.

Smiling wolfishly, Hairless Joe reached for his gun and pointed it at Aiden's chest.

In an act of total desperation, Meg picked up the only weapon available to her — the ashes of Theodore Schuyler, deceased since 1957. Without pausing for either thought or aim, she hurled the metal urn at the assassin's pistol hand.

It was a direct hit. Hairless Joe cried out in pain. The gun clattered to the stone floor. Meg leaped for it, scooped it up, and backed away to stand with her brother.

Through his relief, Aiden understood this moment with sudden perfect clarity and wonder. This was what they had talked about after the near miss with Hairless Joe at the elevator shaft. Meg's own words: *You can't tell me we're not better off if that guy's dead.*

Now the chance was right here. It was time to re-move the threat of Hairless Joe for good and always. For their sake, but for their parents' as well. Danger to Aiden and Meg equaled danger to their quest — and to Mom and Dad's only hope for a future.

His sister just had to pull the trigger.

"Meg — "

"I hear you." Her message had never been tougher, yet her voice belonged to the sixth-grader that she was still supposed to be.

Of all the things this misadventure had de-manded of eleven-year-old Meg Falconer, surely this was the most terrible. Her entire body was trem-bling, except for the hand that held the gun. That was rock steady.

To their surprise, Hairless Joe seemed to relax. "You don't have the nerve." His voice was harsh and mocking. His sneer was ugly, half closing one eye and revealing long, crooked teeth. One of them had a chip out of it.

Aiden's fevered brain labored to make the connection. The chipped tooth . . . Oznot's sketchbook . . .

All at once, he was leaping in front of Meg. *"No!"*

In that fraction of a second, Hairless Joe made a decision of his own. He spun on his heel and was out the door in a heartbeat, leaping off the steps and pounding through the tombstones. There could be no doubt in his mind that he was running for his life.

By the time Meg got to the door, the man was fifty yards away. She rounded on her brother. "Are you crazy? I was going to do it!"

Aiden grabbed his sister by the shoulders as their enemy escaped on foot. "Meg — we can't kill him! We need him!"

She stared. *"Need* him?"

Aiden nodded, shattered with emotion.

"Hairless Joe is Frank Lindenauer."

21

Meg gawked at her brother as if he had just announced that the professional assassin was Elvis.

"What are you talking about? Why would you say that?"

"Because it's true," he insisted. "That's what Oznot was trying to tell us. The sketch of Uncle Frank and the sketch of Hairless Joe — they're the same guy. In the drawing, Frank Lindenauer had a chipped tooth. I just saw that same tooth on Hairless Joe!"

She was unconvinced. "But they look nothing like each other!"

"He had tons of hair and a full beard," Aiden argued urgently. "If you shave all that off, you change your appearance completely! He probably did it when HORUS got busted and he needed to disappear fast. Then he started getting rid of all the people who could expose him — people like Edith Wilkinson. And when he heard we'd escaped from

Sunnydale, he knew we were a threat. So he came after us!"

She was struck dumb. It sounded like the wildest fiction — something straight out of Mac Mulvey. And yet it answered so many questions about the mysterious bald killer who'd been stalking them. How had he tracked them to the lake house in Vermont? Because he'd visited there with the Falconer family. How had he created a poster of "Uncle Frank" to lure them in? Because he was using an old picture of himself. How could he anticipate their every move? Because he knew exactly who they were and what they were trying to do.

And it solved the biggest mystery of all: Why had nobody found Frank Lindenauer, the only person who could clear John and Louise Falconer of treason? Because Frank Lindenauer had become another person.

It was an earthshaking revelation, a discovery that turned reality on its ear. The man they were after was the same man who was after them.

"We're such idiots," she moaned. "It was staring us right in the face. We knew Hairless Joe was a HORUS guy who wasn't arrested with the rest of them. Why didn't we put two and two together?"

"It's hard to think straight when you're hanging over an elevator shaft," Aiden said feelingly.

"Yeah, but we *had* him," Meg persisted. "And we let him get away!"

"*We* have to get away," Aiden reminded her. All around them, the sirens — dozens of them — seemed to be closing in. They counted at least three helicopters in the air.

Meg forced herself to be all business. "The Corvette! You think it's still drivable?"

"I doubt it," Aiden replied. "Otherwise, Hairless Joe would have taken it. But it's worth a try."

Meg hurled the gun as far as she could into the bushes, and the Falconers ran to the scene of the collision between car and tombstone. The closer they got, the deeper Meg's heart sank. The Corvette was a write-off, its front end bashed in, its windshield shattered, fluids leaking from a ruined chassis.

The sound of the voice made them both jump. Had the police already found them?

Then they heard the words: *This is the OnStar operator. We received a signal that your driver airbag has deployed. We have dispatched police and ambulance to the scene.*

"OnStar?" Meg repeated.

"Who's that?" came the voice from the car. *"Is somebody there? Can you hear me?"*

"The police know where we are?" Aiden asked in alarm.

"We've reported your location," the operator confirmed. *"Are you hurt? Is there someone else we can call for you?"*

Meg stiffened like a pointer. "What, you make phone calls, too?"

"Of course. Your OnStar operates as a telephone."

"Good," she said. "Dial one-eight-hundred-U-S M-O-U-T-H."

Aiden goggled. "The Mouth of America? What are you doing? We have to get out of here!"

"He said he'd help us," she replied. "We need help."

The call screener came on. "Mouth line. What's your beef?"

"It's Meg Falconer."

The delay was no more than a few scrambling seconds. The famous voice came out of the OnStar speaker.

"Meg? Are you okay? What's going on with you guys?"

Meg leaned over the ruined hood, projecting

through the empty space where the windshield had once been. "You said you'd help us. Did you mean it?"

"The Mouth is as good as his word," the shock jock told her. "Just name it."

"We're at the Centennial Acres Cemetery in Denver," she began.

Aiden shot her a horrified look for revealing their whereabouts to millions of listeners. Meg ignored him. Secrecy was hardly the issue. Scores of police cars were out looking for them. And OnStar had just pinpointed their exact position by GPS.

"There are a million cops out there and we've got to disappear! Can you help us?"

In reply, the Mouth of America addressed his vast radio audience: "Listen up, everybody in Denver. If you're a fan of this show, it's because you believe in cutting through the garbage, exposing the phonies and idiots, and not letting the almighty powers that be dump all over the little guy. People say we're just hot air. Now's our chance to prove them wrong! How are we going to help these kids?"

"We need an extraction!" Aiden piped up suddenly.

The Mouth was all over that. "Aiden, right? What kind of extraction? What do you mean?"

"*Dead Is a Four-Letter Word* — it's a book by our father. Mac Mulvey's trapped inside this building that's controlled by the Russian mob. So he calls for a team to come and pluck him out. That's an extraction."

"Can do," said the Mouth. "Let me put you on hold."

"No!" screamed Meg, the sirens howling closer around them. "There's not enough time — "

But the shock jock was already gone.

Aiden ripped open the driver door, turned the key in the ignition, switched on the radio, and tuned it to the Mouth of America show.

The Mouth was a notorious ranter. But he was in rare form today, bellowing across the airwaves, haranguing his Denver-area listeners to get in their cars and give the fugitive Falconers a lift.

Meg was wound up like a coiled spring. "You think he can make this happen?"

"Get down!" Aiden took hold of her shoulders, and the two of them dropped behind the Corvette.

A police car was driving slowly along the cemetery's main path. The officer peered out his window, scanning the grounds.

It's only a matter of time before he spots the Corvette, Meg thought with sickening resignation.

At that moment, the voice returned from the On-Star system — not the Mouth, but the radio show's call screener. "Can you hear me, kids? There should be a gate at the east entrance. There's an angel with wings on top of the fence. Wait for a gray Chevy Malibu. Good luck!"

Bent double, they set their sights on the winged angel and ran. As they darted from tombstone to tombstone, staying low, they watched the cemetery fill up with squad cars.

There was a sudden burst of excited voices and running feet. Meg peered out from behind a marble marker. The cops were descending in force on the wreckage of the Corvette.

Thirty seconds sooner and we'd have been standing right there!

The east gate was about a thousand yards away. It felt like fifty miles. Their backs ached from their squatting posture and the tension brought on by fear of discovery. Every inch of the way, they braced themselves against the cry that might come — *"There they are!"* By the time they were at last crouching amid the concealing branches of a juniper bush just inside the gate, they were sweat-soaked and trembling.

Meg peered out past the pillars to the road. No gray Malibu.

"Do you think we missed him?" she whispered.

"He'd wait," Aiden replied.

They both hoped that was true.

"Are we nuts to get into some stranger's car?" she asked timidly. "I mean, not knowing anything else about the person except he listens to the radio?"

"Sure, we're nuts. But we'd be more nuts to stay here."

A midsize gray Chevy drew up to the curb. A click signified the release of automatic door locks.

"This is it!" Aiden hissed. "One, two, three!" They burst out of the shelter of the bushes, hit the sidewalk with a bound, and jumped into the back of the Malibu. The car pulled away from the curb.

Lying low on the seat, the two could barely catch their breath.

"Thanks, mister," Aiden gasped.

"Don't sweat it," said the driver, a long-haired young man with a ponytail tucked inside a Denver Broncos cap. He swung an arm back and handed Meg a cell phone. "The Mouth wants to talk to you."

Meg was barely able to come up with the word hello.

"Good — you made it," approved the shock jock's familiar voice. "Okay, we've got seven cars on the road. We're going to hand you off a few times to make sure you're not being followed."

As Centennial Acres fell away from the rear window, police cruisers continued to converge on the cemetery. Officers were establishing roadblocks at the gates, and helicopters hovered over the grounds.

All at once, the strain of the past hours caught up with Meg — the high-speed chase, the confrontation with a murderer, and the murder she herself had very nearly committed. Now this escape from the police — helped by strangers commanded by a man who had once called for their parents' execution.

Sudden tears stung her eyes. "Mr. Mouth," she quavered, "I don't know how we're ever going to thank you!"

For the second time in his career, the Mouth of America was speechless.

22

When Agent Harris reached the cemetery, the search was over. It had produced one stolen motorcycle, one wrecked Corvette, and a nine-millimeter pistol that was already on its way to the crime lab.

Harris flashed his FBI identification. "What's going on? Where do we stand?"

The lieutenant on the scene was one of a group of officers standing around the Corvette. "Near as we can tell, the kids ran out of gas on the Harley and ditched it. We don't know who was driving the 'vette, but he must have a head like a cannonball if he walked away from this collision."

Harris nodded. "A big bald head. He's trying to kill those kids."

"Maybe we can lift his prints off the gun," the lieutenant said hopefully. "That's all we've got, except a dented urn full of ashes. We think the kids might have fought him off with it."

Harris was agitated. "Why'd you stop the search? They were here twenty minutes ago!"

"They're miles away."

"How can you be so sure?" Harris insisted. "This is a huge cemetery, with lots of places to hide."

In answer, the lieutenant reached down and clicked on the car radio.

"This is what it's all about, people!" the Mouth was shouting. "Talk may be cheap, but nobody can say we weren't ready to step up to the plate today! Thanks to our Denver listeners, Aiden and Meg Falconer are free right now! Good luck, you guys — we're all cheering for you! That's how I see it! You got a problem with that?"

Agent Emmanuel Harris had a problem with that.

Aiden and Meg had been on the move for several hours, with six different drivers in six different cars. The exchanges had been random and completely unexpected, taking place under bridges, in tunnels, and in covered parking lots, just in case they were being tracked by helicopter. It was meticulously or-chestrated by the Mouth and his staff from two thousand miles away in New York. Suddenly, a cell phone would be handed over the seat, and the shock jock would say, "Red Nissan Pathfinder — go!"

And like magic, there the car would be, parked and waiting for them.

It was getting dark. They were a couple of hours outside the city, in a white Ford Taurus driven by a tough-looking middle-aged woman who worked nights repossessing cars.

By this time, it was clear that the "extraction" was a success. No one was following them, and the Denver dragnet was a hundred miles or more in the Taurus's rearview mirror. Yet the feeling of relief was far from joyous. They still had no place to go, no money, and no clear way to help Mom and Dad. This wasn't victory — it was squeaking through, battered and bloody, staving off the end of the world for one more day.

So why was Aiden feeling so absurdly happy? It was as if a huge burden had been lifted from his shoulders, and he was floating, lighter than air. He felt like singing.

But all the burdens were still in place, heavier than ever.

Am I losing my mind? I have nothing to celebrate!

He did, though, and it was this: Unlike Meg, he

had always been racked by doubt. What if Mom and Dad really were traitors? Now they knew that Frank Lindenauer and Hairless Joe were one and the same. That simple fact blew away the fog that had been surrounding the truth. The man who had framed their parents was eliminating all possible witnesses to cover up his own terrible crimes.

Mom and Dad had committed no crimes at all.

Of course, Aiden had always believed that — always wanted to believe it. But knowing it for certain made his heart soar.

"What are you grinning about?" Meg grumbled. "Mac Mulvey didn't extract us, the Mouth did."

The shock jock's voice rang out over the Taurus's radio. Their savior was still on the air, hours after his scheduled program had ended. Thousands of phone calls, pro and con, had been pouring in all day, and the Mouth had pledged to stick around to listen to every single opinion.

The current caller had Aiden and Meg hanging on his every word. It was Agent Emmanuel Harris, and he was red-hot steaming mad over what the Mouth had done.

"It's not a public service, it's a federal crime! Freedom of the press doesn't cover aiding and abetting fugitives! If you don't identify your accomplices and help us bring in those kids, I can have you prosecuted to the full extent of the law!"

The Mouth was defiant. "Is that the kind of justice you were practicing when you dumped them on a prison farm after your kangaroo court convicted their parents?"

That obviously stung. "I've reopened the Falconers' case. The files are on my desk, and I'd be reviewing them *this minute* if some misguided fool wasn't moving heaven and earth to keep those children out on their own, in harm's way!"

In the back of the Taurus, Aiden and Meg exchanged a look of wonder. Could that be true? Was the FBI really reconsidering their parents' conviction?

No words passed between them, but both arrived at exactly the same conclusion. Anything that came out of Agent Harris's mouth wasn't worth the air it took to carry the sound waves. It was just another trick to get them to turn themselves in.

The Mouth thought so, too. "You ought to be ashamed of yourself, Harris. We can all sleep soundly knowing our government is protecting us by hounding two defenseless kids. Get off my radio show! Go beat up a baby or something!" He pulled the plug on the FBI agent and cut to a commercial.

A few seconds later, the cell phone rang. The woman put it on speaker.

"How are you doing, guys? Everything okay?" The Mouth didn't wait for an answer. "You're about to be dropped off at a small-town bus station. Your driver's going to give you some money. Buy your tickets from the machine, not the counter. And don't let anybody know where you're going — not your driver, not even me. Got it?"

Meg spoke up. "If we ever get our lives straightened out, we'll make this up to you. We'll tell the world what you did for us. And we'll come on your show and give you a big exclusive."

"And we'll pay you back every cent," Aiden put in.

"I may be a little hard to track down for the foreseeable future," the shock jock said in an odd voice. "I think I'm going to be arrested pretty soon."

"Sorry," mumbled Meg.

"We'll never forget how you stuck your neck out for us," added Aiden.

"Don't worry about me," the shock jock shrugged it off. "I get thrown in jail every time the wind blows. It's good PR for the show. I should be thanking *you* guys. The problem with talk radio — it's just talk. But every now and then something comes along that reminds you what's really important. You kids are so busy staying alive that you probably don't even notice. The way you're fighting for your family — it makes me proud to be human! That's how I see it. You got a problem with that?"

"No problem at all," Meg said hoarsely. But the connection was already broken.

A few minutes later, they were let off at a general store that also served as a bus depot. The driver pressed two hundred dollars into Aiden's hand, ordered him to look after his little sister, and sped off in the direction they'd come from.

Standing at the side of the road, watching the Taurus disappear, Meg heaved a world-weary sigh. "What now, bro? We've got bus ticket money, but nowhere to go."

"We're not going anywhere," he replied. "We've been looking for Frank Lindenauer. Well, today we found him."

"We found him a long time ago," his sister pointed out. "Today was the day we put a name to the ugly face."

"We can't go back to Denver just yet," Aiden went on. "Not till things cool off. But that's where he is, so that's where we have to be."

She was dismayed. "It's a little more complicated

than that, Aiden. He may be our target, but we're *his* targets, too! He's trying to kill us. We can't run toward him and away from him at the same time!"

"That's why we have to set a trap."

She was skeptical. "Using what as bait?"

Aiden squared his jaw. The plan had been forming in his mind ever since it had become clear that their escape from the cemetery was going to be successful. It would be tricky and lethally dangerous. But the time had come to risk everything for a chance to save the Falconer family.

"*We're* the bait."

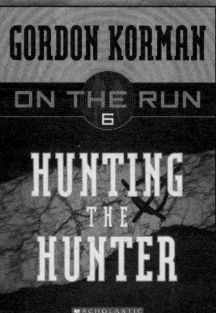

SWIM. CLIMB. DIVE.
GO ON MORE THRILLING ADVENTURES WITH GORDON KORMAN!

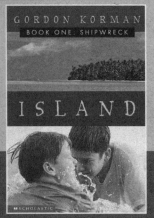

Island

Six troubled teenagers fight for survival after being shipwrecked on a desert island. Can they rise above their own conflicts and work together to stay alive?

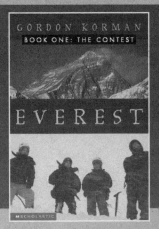

Everest

Who will be the youngest teen to ever climb Everest? And what will happen when disaster strikes?

Dive

Four young divers try to salvage sunken treasure without becoming shark bait. Are they in over their heads?

www.scholastic.com

📖 SCHOLASTIC

GKT